STARSHIP MOONHAWK™
How to Steal a Starship

Michael C. Prokop

Moonhawk Publishing™
www.starshipmoonhawk.com

"One ship stands between
order and chaos."
Tucson, AZ

Starship Moonhawk™: How to Steal a Starship
Copyright © 2016 Michael Prokop

ISBN-10: 0692674349
ISBN-13: 978-0692674345 (Moonhawk Publishing)

Moonhawk Publishing
62053 E. Redwood Dr.
Tucson, AZ 85739

First Moonhawk Publishing paperback printing: March 2016
First Moonhawk Publishing electronic printing: March 2016

Visit Starship Moonhawk on the web at
http://www.starshipmoonhawk.com.

Cover art by Jamie Jennings

Chapter 1

The ship was a technological wonder to behold. It was a sight that most human beings would never see up close, but due to the Crysallis destroying the Jupiter Shipyards several months ago, the mighty mile long dreadnought was hove to for repairs at the old Naval shipyards in Norfolk, Virginia. The space fortress was so massive; it could almost be seen from orbit.

As things stood, the ancient headquarters of the United States Navy's submarine fleet in the Atlantic was the only yard with the equipment and the resources to do the job. The titanic starship was landed here for repairs after her recent run-in with the Fezzini *Ketlet* class battle cruiser.

Wow, she actually floats, the shadowy figure thought. He eyed the prize hungrily. He knew that it would only be a matter of hours now. He could see how the massive scaffolding, both archaic and hover pod gangplanks, made a spider web latticework over the hull of the gigantic vessel. He wondered silently to himself how many precision welds were in a ship so great. He wondered how many rivets and metal plates comprised her skin. Thousands upon thousands of man-hours put into creating such a magnificent piece of machinery... and he was going to steal it in precisely thirty minutes.

The figure checked his chrono. Oh-two twenty-eight. Two minutes to go. The acids in his stomach churned with anxiety. He had done this several times before, but never on such a grand scale. Ironically, this kind of infiltration could not have been done in space. The ship would have been scanning for trouble, and thieves in space suits and shuttles would have been picked up on radar almost instantly. Fortunately for these thieves, the ship was here, on the surface. It was an occurrence that only happened once in a generation, possibly even less frequently than that. *Fortunate indeed that it happened during MY lifetime,* he thought.

He checked his chrono again. Oh-two thirty on the dot. He let out a quick whistle and the game was on. Several other figures emerged from the shadows and made their way to the gangplank. Within moments they had subdued the guards with professional skill. He smiled inwardly with pride at the level of ability his people exhibited. Not a sound was heard. He hopped down from his vantage point and made his way across the wharf. He reached the gangplank and had to suppress the urge to gasp. The ship was taller than the Sears Tower in Chicago. He almost fell from the vertigo, but one of his cohorts caught his arm and pushed him back up.

"I'm just not used to the size up close," he said, casually.

"Affirmative," came the whispered reply.

They arrived at the airlock and the suited woman

next to him produced a device from a pouch in her wetsuit and placed it on the door. She pointed with her index and forefingers at her eyes made a sweeping motion encompassing the small party and pointed toward the door. All nodded in understanding. She keyed in a sequence on the pad. *Breee-oop!* Nothing happened. She scratched her head, then keyed in the sequence again. *Breee-oop!* Same results.

"C'mon, quit fucking around," the hooded man whispered tersely.

"I'm not. They changed the code... hold on, let me try something."

She keyed a new sequence in; this one caused the door to make a different noise. Suddenly the bolt gave way and the door slid open with a small whoosh. They could smell the difference in air quality inside. The air was slightly metallic. They knew it was actually cleaner than the "fresh" air they were breathing on the outside, but it still seemed a little unnatural.

The five figures entered the portal. The corridor was empty, which was as expected. Most of the two thousand crewmembers were on extended shore leave while the repair crews were working on the *Moonhawk*. At this time of night there was only a minimal security team on board. *Should be easy enough to dispatch*, the man thought. After all, this was what he was trained for. He turned the next corridor and made his way to the lift that would take them topside. At the doors he stopped and turned to the people.

"All right, listen up. This is it. Number four and five, you head to the security control station. We'll strike the security detail on the bridge. Once you get there, wait for our signal. When we have control of the security systems, we can dispatch the remaining personnel on the ship with gas. Victory is within our grasp."

They all nodded assent. *A little melodramatic,* he thought, *but it served its purpose.* Four and five headed down the corridor to the lift that would take them to the security complex. The remaining three piled into the lift. As the doors slid shut Number One wondered how good their intelligence was. *Well, I guess we're gonna find out soon enough.*

Commander Sorthac and Lt. Commander Rachael Harrison sat staring intently at one another. Neither one dared to move. They could feel the intensity rising, the tension mounting. Rachael reached up and wiped a tiny bead of perspiration from her forehead. She acted first.

"I call."

"Are you certain you do not wish to reconsider? There is no shame in a tactical retreat."

"I'm sure."

"Very well, Rachael. I have a full house. Aces over eight's." *A decidedly first-rate hand,* he complimented himself. He tried to read her expression as he reached over to collect the chips in the pot.

"I'm sorry, sir, but I'm afraid I can't let you take that," she added gravely after a moment of consideration. "Unfortunately, four deuces is still four-of-a-kind and beats a full house."

Sorthac stared for a moment in disbelief. How can this be! Deuces were the worst cards to have, and yet having all of them from the deck gave one an almost unbeatable hand!

"You must have cheated!"

"What? Sorthac, are you out of your scaly skull? Why would I cheat? We're not even playing for real money," she insisted. "Gambling on duty is in direct violation of regulations!"

"Then how do you explain that incredible stroke of luck you have had all night?" He demanded.

"I don't know Sorthac, that's why they call it luck. *It's random*."

"This is a game unworthy of a warrior. It is a game of lies and deception."

"You are impossible, Sorthac. C'mon, let's play Gin Rummy instead."

"No. I do not wish to play any more of these foolish card games."

"Look, don't be such a big baby about losing. These games weren't foolish when you won five straight hands."

"Well I had no reason to suspect you were cheating then. Now I know the truth."

"Wow, Commander. If this is how you treat your friends, I would hate to meet your enemies."

"My *male* friends would not be suspect."

"I'm going to the head."

"Fine. Don't let me stop you. I'm just your commanding officer. Nobody important."

She waved her hand back at him in a dismissive gesture and made an unpleasant face. *Yeah, and maybe when I get back from the head you'll have yours out of your ass,* she thought. She was actually very fond of Sorthac, and she also had a great deal of respect for him. She would never be so familiar with him in the presence of other personnel. These times when they were pulling all night security duty were different. They could be more themselves since there was nobody around to see them. She used to wonder why Sorthac would insist that they pull these shifts instead of delegating them to lesser ranked or experienced persons, but she came to a realization: either Sorthac was sweet on her and wanted her alone as much as possible, or he really never slept. In which case his only goal was to make sure that she never did either.

She climbed down the stairs to the level just below the bridge where the facilities were. *Ooooooh!* She thought. *I have to go worse than I had originally thought*, and darted inside.

Sorthac stared at the cards laid out on the table.

There was no way that she could have beaten him in that manner fairly... could she? He examined the cards looking for some evidence that she had cheated, but as he actually had suspected, there was none. He knew in his heart that she had not cheated, and he regretted his childish accusations. After all, he *was* the seasoned officer. Out of frustration he pushed the cards off of the makeshift card table they had made out of the science station and they scattered on the deck below. He picked up the poker chips and placed them back in the secret compartment in the back of the chair. He was about to pick up the cards when he noticed the sound of the lift approaching the bridge level.

Strange, he thought. *We aren't supposed to be relieved for at least another hour*.

He placed his hand tentatively on his sidearm. The lift stopped. Sorthac was ready to draw when the lift doors suddenly opened revealing an empty car.

"Hmm," he said aloud. "I guess we'll have to have the maintenance crews check for bugs in the lift system's electronic sensors."

Then the ceiling crashed down on him. Rather, one of the panels from the ceiling was on top of him. He only had a split second before he realized that he was not alone. He rolled his bulk and narrowly missed the butt of the rifle coming down where he was just moments before. He kicked out with his left foot and struck the assailants leg. He heard a woman yelp in pain. He flipped and twisted his massive self behind the radar console. Sparks flew off of the metal trim where a pulse rifle blast struck the edge. Two small streams of smoke pirouetted from the marks. He finally drew his own firearm but it was knocked clear by the another assailant from behind. The foolish attacker tried to grapple Sorthac in a Full Nelson. Sorthac grinned that peculiar lizard grin. In a contest of pure brute force, few could stand against him. He broke the hold with a sharp elbow to the man's rib cage. He heard a satisfying crack as the blow struck home. The attacker staggered backward in obvious pain. He was gasping for air. That was when the pulse bolt struck him in the leg. Sorthac doubled over and grabbed the smoldering spot near his knee. The pain and smell of burning scales made his stomach turn, but he resolved not to give his attackers the satisfaction of seeing him vomit.

"What do you want?" He hissed through his clenched teeth.

"I want you to surrender your vessel, Commander," the masked figure stated without preamble.

"You'll have to take it over my dead body."

"Fortunately for you, that won't be necessary, Mr. Sorthac."

"How do you know who I am? Who are you," demanded Sorthac.

The hooded man took off his mask and showed his face for the first time. He was about six feet tall. He had dusty brown hair and piercing blue eyes. He had an angular face and a dimple in his chin, but no facial growth. He looked about thirty-ish, but the lines around his eyes made him look like he was about two hundred years old to Sorthac. He couldn't figure out why this young man looked so damn familiar.

"If it really matters to you that much, Commander Sorthac, you may call me Jason, and this is Sam and Jerry." The other two pulled their masks off. Sorthac could see now that the woman (now sporting a rather interesting limp) was five-seven and had almost burgundy hair with dark brown eyes, she was rather attractive as far as human females were concerned. The man indicated as Jerry (Who was clinging gingerly onto his rib cage) was around five-eleven and was graying near the temples. His face was taut, and his build was muscular, like a marine. His haircut matched the description because it was close cropped.

"Now, Commander, I'm afraid it is lights out time. You have been a terrible inconvenience, and your presence here on the bridge cannot be tolerated."

The butt of the woman's rifle came around and stuck him in the back of the neck. The last thing he saw was the smiling face of the one called Jason and Sorthac burned that face into his memory before unconsciousness finally claimed him.

Chapter 2

Rachael Harrison looked at herself in the mirror of the unisex restroom as she washed her hands in the sink. The sonic waves that were designed to remove dirt were soothing on her hands.

"Water, warm," she ordered the sink. Warm water poured over her palms. She cupped them together and collected the liquid. She splashed some on her face. She was getting tired, and she could see in her reflection the fatigue lines appearing around the edges of her eyes. *Serves me right for letting Sorthac talk me into pulling a double shift*, she thought ruefully.

She walked over to the air dryer and was about to press the button when she heard pulse rifle blasts from above.

The sound was followed quickly by a series of crashes and the muffled yelp of a woman. There was obviously some kind of struggle going on above. Rachael wasted no time. She quickly dried her hands on her pants and began looking for an alternate form of egress. Doubtless when the assailants were finished with Sorthac, they would be after her next. Even if they weren't immediately suspicious, they would soon remember that the Navy regulations made security details operate in pairs. Then they would start looking for the missing guard, namely her. She saw the air circulation duct in the ceiling above the rear stall, whipped the door open and climbed up the toilet to work the grating off. She flipped the latch and the grating swung open. She grabbed the handholds and hoisted herself into the opening. Finally, she closed the grate just behind her just in time to hear one of the intruders make their way down the stairs to the head. She remained motionless for a moment.

The perpetrator moved slowly into view of the grating. Rachael could see that it was a woman with burgundy hair carrying a hefty pulse rifle. The woman stopped and scanned the room visually looking one way, then the other. Rachael wasn't sure if the woman had heard her clambering into the duct before she got to the room. She tried to control her breathing. She also had to resist the urge to jump down from her hiding place and pummel the woman. *Won't be much good to Sorthac or anyone else if I'm captured or dead*, she thought.

The woman lingered a little longer. She must suspect something, Rachael thought. She turned slowly, still listening and hobbled a little bit as she made her way toward the door. *I wonder how many of them there are*, she thought to herself.

She lucked out since the intruder didn't scan for her presence with any kind of electronic scanning device. *Kinda sloppy*, she mused. Even though he didn't completely dispatch them, she imagined that Sorthac put up quite a fight. That meant that the intruders weren't at full capacity, but she was. She looked down the length of the ductwork she was in and muttered under her breath.

"Of all the times not to have a map."

"I thought you said this would be easy!"

"Sam, I thought I told you to shut the hell up about it, already!"

"Well, Jerry, you were the one that said that this would be a piece of cake. 'No problem', you said. It'll be like stealing candy from a baby,' you said. 'They would never expect someone to steal the ship from planetside, security will be minimal,' you said. HAH!"

Jerry brought his hand back as if to strike her.

"Jerry, you would actually strike an officer," she said mockingly.

"Enough!"

Both of them looked at Jason.

"This bickering will get us nowhere. Five people will get us off of Earth, but once we launch, we will only be able to control the ship for seven hours before we lose control of the automated systems. After that point, we will need a crew of no less than one hundred fifty. We have to make the rendezvous before that deadline."

The others nodded in agreement.

"Sam, send the signal to our other team. They are probably worried by now."

"Got it, Jason." She turned and moved to the tactical station.

"Sir, what do we do with him?" Jerry indicated to Sorthac lying on the floor.

"Place him in the brig with the rest of the security personnel we find along the way. I want them to be closely monitored."

"Aye, sir." He began to drag Sorthac with some considerable effort.

"Sir, we have neutralized the remaining security teams by using the anti-intruder gas," Sam reported.

"Excellent. Let's get to our stations."

The duo set to work taking control of steerage. Jason took the helm and Sam took control of the Operations console.

"Clear all moorings."

"Moorings, aye."

The tractor beams that served as moorings cleared the ship one by one. At this hour, people would notice the running lights of the massive space fortress coming online, but at the base it was gamma shift, the lightest shift of the day, so response time would be sluggish at best.

"Bring main thrusters online."

"Thrusters, aye."

"The giant thruster jets of the huge vessel fired several times and the ship began to rise out of the water. The sudden change in displacement caused several large waves to crash against the wharf. Several of the warehouses were blown over in the sudden pressure change under the giant turbines. Alarm klaxons began to wail, but most of them could not be heard over the whooshing sound. It was as though someone had turned on a mile long vacuum cleaner. The engines roared under the stress. Gravity was trying to assert itself.

"Watch your trim, helm. Let's get this crate off the ground."

The starship angled slightly as it made its ascent. The comm channel came to life suddenly.

"To the unidentified pilots, this launch is not authorized. Shut down your engines and return to the surface immediately. Respond."

"Ignore them. We have bigger problems."

The dreadnought angled sharper toward the sky and the ascent accelerated.

Admiral William Eubanks didn't like being rousted out of bed before 0500 hours. It robbed him of what he referred to as his 'beauty sleep'. He liked the sound of the alert klaxons even less, which only served to hasten his pace.

When he arrived at the command center everything was in chaos. Ensigns and Chiefs were crashing into one another everyone was talking excitedly and at the same time. He put on his hat and waded into the mess.

"Admiral on deck!"

"Day late and a dollar short, petty officer," he snarled. "Give me a status report, now!"

A nondescript ensign came forward with a pad. "Sir, someone is stealing the starship *Moonhawk*," he stated nervously.

"Is this some kind of prank?"

"No sir! See for yourself, sir."

The ensign brought up a tactical display on the main holo viewer. It showed the *Moonhawk* making a steady climb for the atmosphere.

"Get me the *Hornet* and the *Wasp* in orbit. Move your butt Ensign, like it already happened!"

"Aye sir!"

The Ensign activated some controls on the console. After a few seconds he looked up at the Admiral.

"I have the *Hornet* and *Wasp* standing by, Admiral."

"Jay, Earl, I don't have much time. Check your scanners, you're about to have company up there. Stop the starship *Moonhawk*. I repeat STOP the *Moonhawk*. She's been hijacked."

Captain Earl Forrester of the Heavy Cruiser *USAS Wasp* and Captain Jay Casterelli of the Light Cruiser *USAS Hornet* responded in unison: "The *Moonhawk*, sir?" There was a noticeable pause. Captain Forrester was the first to respond. "We're on our way to barricade them in, sir."

The *Moonhawk* cleared the atmosphere of planet Earth without incident. Suddenly the ship's shields registered the first volley from the automated defense systems. The ship vibrated under the barrage.

"This is nothing," Jason noted rather offhandedly. "I remember when we went through BUD/S training they had us ride this old tin can through the orbital defenses, unshielded. It felt like a damn nuclear torpedo hit us when the bombardment started. These turrets won't even scratch the paint off the *Moonhawk*."

"Uh, Jason, I wouldn't be too concerned about *those* turrets if I were you."

"What do you mean '*those*' turrets?"

She didn't even have a chance to respond as the *Wasp* and *Hornet* laced into their shields. The impact threw the two to the deck.

"Holy shit, they must have hit us with full force!" Jason commented picking himself up off the floor. The radio crackled to life again.

"Unidentified pilots, this is your final warning. Turn the *Moonhawk* around, and return it to port, or we have been authorized to top you by *any means necessary*."

The two blinked in surprise for a moment.

"Are they serious, Jason? Would they actually destroy the *Moonhawk*? Even with their people on board? The flagship of the fleet?"

"If it means that the 'enemy' can't get their hands on it, absolutely. That's the risk we all sign up for when we join the Navy."

"Do you think they are bluffing?"

"I'm not going to give them a chance to try." And with that, Jason threw the throttle forward into the 'flank' position.

"What are you doing?!"

"I'm going to play chicken with a couple of cruisers."

"Are you crazy?!"

"Sam, stop shrieking. It's really quite detrimental to my concentration." He wiped a small bead of sweat from his brow. The two cruisers angled toward the battleship like a picket line daring the *Moonhawk* to cross. The bracketing fire continued. The Moonhawk shuddered a little under the pounding. The ships were holding nothing back, but the *Moonhawk's* shields were holding, miraculously.

"We're gonna hit them!"

"Yes, Sam. Again, I am aware of this!"

"But if we collide, the ships will be destroyed!"

"Have faith, Goddamnit Samantha!"

The battleship stormed toward the two cruisers in the biggest game of galactic chicken ever played, neither side giving an inch. The bead of sweat was growing on Jason's face. He had a small flash of doubt in his plan as the gap closed to five thousand kilometers, four, three, two, one...

...And the two other ships veered sharply. Not sharply enough. The *Moonhawk's* shields struck the shields of the other two ships, but not directly. The glancing blow was enough to knock both of the smaller vessels off course. They shot away from the *Moonhawk* like Ping-Pong balls. The *Wasp*, being the larger ship, was able to absorb some of the collision and correct it's course, engines straining to avoid having the ship spiral out of control. The *Hornet*, being smaller fared far worse. One of the engine pods at the rear of the ship exploded, causing the other engines to sputter and die. The ship began delisting and tumbled away like a rag doll being discarded. The *Moonhawk* continued on it's way without losing speed.

"There, see? Nothing to worry about. They'll survive."

"Christ, Jason! Don't do that! You almost killed them *and* us!"

"I seriously doubt it, although, those guys on the *Hornet* won't be going anywhere for a while."

"SEALs are all the same. *Completely NUTS!*"

"Don't forget, you're one of us now." She was still looking at him with barely contained fury.

"Well, Samantha, look at it this way. When this is all over, they won't soon forget that we stole Admiral Gil Cobalt's ship. Now let's keep our eyes on the ball. After the rendezvous, we have two days hard travel to our destination. We have no time to waste." They activated the Dimensional Doorway system and completed their escape.

"Sir, they are escaping!"

"I can see that, Lieutenant." The Admiral was thoughtful for a second before he spoke again. "Contact..." he consulted the sector board for the nearest starship in intercept range. "The *U.S.S. Galahad*. She's the closest ship." And then he added after a second of thought: "And find me Admiral Cobalt. After all, he is the captain of that damn monstrosity!"

Chapter 3

Captain Neriah Solis didn't really mind waiting. She had time on her hands more often than she could count. She felt that someone in her position should be busier. This actually disturbed her more than the fact that she was sitting on a park bench outside the Naval Command Center on Earth.

Truth be told, she hadn't visited Earth in over 15 years since her father died in the Two-Decade War. He was an operative for Naval Intelligence. The risks were part of the job. Neriah knew this, but for some reason her homeworld seemed cold comfort. She was an Outsider. She hated the name. It suggested that humanity considered them to be something else. *Not one of us,* she mused silently.

She actually liked these moments of calm where she could collect herself quietly and retune herself with nature. The chirping birds and the cool Atlantic breeze were her mantra. She had forgotten how the sounds of the Eastern seaboard relaxed her. It was unusually inactive outside Naval Space Command for a weekday. She closed her eyes and let herself go for a moment. She released all of her concerns and let the stress of her position as executive officer and Commander Airspace Group of the Starship *Moonhawk* fade away.

She focused on one the seagulls swooping and

diving over the surf without a care in the world. She imagined that she was one of them, spreading her wings and fluttering in the breeze. She could see the other birds squawking as they dove into the cool azure waters to fish. She coasted on the wind momentarily and fell into step with the flock, careening high above the now seemingly insignificant worries of the land below. *This is living*, she thought. *This is freedom*. She continued higher into the clouds and deftly executed another dive. The lift caught under her wings and brought her up again gently. One of the other gulls veered toward her, almost on collision course. It's shadow seemed to somehow envelop her even though she had deftly avoided its advance. The other gull was no longer moving. It was hovering right in front of her, looking at her. She jumped almost instinctively and snapping out of her trance found herself staring into the warm blue eyes of Admiral Gilliad Cobalt, her friend and commanding officer. He plunked himself down and draped himself rather nonchalantly across the bench.

"Miss me?" He asked with a touch of humor in his voice.

"You shouldn't sneak up on someone in a trance, sir. It's hazardous."

"I'll try to keep that in mind," he laughed. There was something different about him. He was usually very serious, reserved even, after a session with the Navy commanders. She just looked at him for a second not saying anything, and then she saw it. On the shoulder boards of his summer whites where he formerly had only gold bars, he now had two black pipes attached in the front and back. She blinked in surprise.

"What happened?"

"We were promoted!"

"'We', sir?"

Cobalt still wearing his winningest smile reached into his pocket and produced a small black jewelry box. He handed it to Solis.

"Gil, you're not proposing to me are you?"

He laughed a hearty laugh. "No no no, Neriah. I couldn't do that. We're in the same command and that's against the rules! Open it."

She wasn't sure why, but she was disappointed to hear that. She opened the box anyway. Inside it lay two golden suns with no pip, apparently a matched pair. The breath caught in her throat.

"I won't be needing those anymore, so I wanted you to have them," he said.

"Gil, I don't know what to say."

"How about 'thank you, sir.' I've found that works quite nicely."

"Thank you, sir!"

"Forget about it. You deserve it, *Commodore* Solis. Your father would have been proud." He regretted the words even as they came out of his mouth. "Neriah, I'm sorry, I didn't mean..."

"No, it's all right Gil. I have to face the demons

of my past. I can't run from Earth forever." She was silent for a moment.

"Well, I apologize for spoiling the moment at any rate, but he *would* have been proud. *And*, you are the first Outsider to ever attain Flag rank."

She looked at him sharply. "Gil, this had better not be--"

"Whoa, put the safety back on. It's not like that. I'm now commander of the First Fleet, so they asked me who I wanted to promote to be my Chief of Operations."

"Was I *first* on the list?"

"Ouch. That was cold. Of *course* you were. You were the *only* name on the list." He tried to fake a look of admonishment, but failed as they both broke out in a small fit of laughter.

BEEP BEEP!

"Was that you, or me, Gil?"

BEEP BEEP!

"It's has to be you. I turned mine off for the meeting this morning."

Solis shot him a look. "Great. They could have been paging you for hours, and you would have had no idea what is going on," she said with mild annoyance. "Nine-one-one. What does that mean, Gil?"

"I think it is a reference to an ancient method of communication called the telephone. This was the code that they used to alert the emergency services that there was trouble," he said.

"We better go."

"Lead the way, *Commodore* Solis."

"You're going to be insufferable about that aren't you?"

"That is my current plan, yes."

She threw up her hands in defeat as they took off for the shuttle port.

"Well, it took you bloody long enough to answer your pages, Admiral! Not very auspicious of a newly promoted two-star." Admiral Eubanks clucked his tongue completing the admonishment. Admiral Cobalt remained silent.

"Good to know that you have *your* locator turned on at all hours Ca--er *Commodore* Solis. Otherwise we would never have found our wayward captain, would we?"

Admiral Cobalt's face turned a new shade of red. His beard didn't hide it very well. Neriah knew that he didn't take being put on the spot like that very well and wisely nodded deferentially toward Admiral Eubanks rather than give voice to her affirmative. She was also acutely aware that Admiral Eubanks was not big on making a public spectacle of his officer's mistakes. She saw the dark circles under the senior admiral's eyes and decided that this out of character behavior was a direct result of sleep deprivation.

"May I ask what is going on here, *sir*?" Cobalt's tone was dangerously close to insubordination.

"Yes, and I would watch my tone if I were you, especially in light of what I am about to tell you next." The admiral walked to the large viewport at the front of the station. "Notice anything missing, Admiral Cobalt?"

Cobalt made his way to the window with Solis close behind. At once he could see the destroyed wharf and the overturned warehouses. They were blown over like dominoes. There were sailors all over the place trying to sift through the wreckage for salvage materials. They reminded Cobalt of ants in his ant farm from childhood.

"What happened here?" He asked.

"Isn't there something wrong with this picture, Admiral? I mean, besides the entire base being leveled."

Solis spoke next. "Sir, I really don't see the point behind the guessing--"

"The *Moonhawk* is gone!" Admiral Cobalt cut in.

Solis stared at the dock where the huge space fortress was moored a mere twelve hours before, but all that remained was open ocean as far as the eye could see and a lot of floating debris from the warehouses. She opened her mouth to speak, but there were no words. She caught herself gaping and quickly closed her mouth.

"How could this happen? *Here* on Earth! We took all of the standard security measures. Everything was set up according to the regs!"

"Gil, how could the regs be observed when the *Moonhawk* being planetside is anything *but* 'regulation'? I'm not bent out of shape with *you* specifically for this disaster, but you *are* going to help us get out of it. *Nobody* knows that ship better than you do, and you're going to help us stop her, even if it means destroying her."

Eubank's last statement resonated throughout the control room.

"Destroy it?"

"If necessary, Gil."

"Sir, I have people aboard that ship."

"Who all signed up knowing full well that their lives could be forfeit any day of the week and you damn well know it," Eubanks snapped.

"Sir, if there is a way to avoid destroying the *Moonhawk*, I will find it," Cobalt stated with determination.

"I'm glad to hear it," Eubanks responded. "You and your staff will meet up with the U.S.S. *Galahad*. She's the biggest ship we have in range to overtake and intercept the *Moonhawk*."

"The *Galahad*, sir?"

"Is there a problem, Admiral?"

"No sir. No problem..."

"Good," said Eubanks continuing the impromptu briefing. "We have no time to waste. We have no idea who the perpetrators are or what they want, so be careful. We'll wait here and see if they make any demands. You have your orders, so get cracking."

With that Cobalt and Solis snapped a quick salute, turned and strode out of the control room leaving

Admiral Eubanks to consider how best to inform the President that the Navy's flagship was stolen right out of their own shipyards.

The shuttle's thrusters propelled it into space. Admiral Cobalt and Commodore Solis sat side-by-side without saying anything. The silence was beginning to irritate Solis.

"Are you going to tell me what the hell that comment was about?"

"What comment?"

"The one about the *Galahad*."

"Oh, that one."

Solis crossed her arms and frowned. "Gil, would you care to elaborate?"

"Not really," he responded simply. He looked at her for the first time since they boarded the shuttle and saw the combination of irritation and frustration in his first officer and friend's face. As powerful a telepath as she was, she could not read his thoughts. He had some kind of mental barrier that most humans did not possess. This was an endless source of frustration for his X-O.

"Well, the truth is, My daughter is in command of that ship."

"Skye?"

"No, Melissa, the older one. Remember the *Galahad* is a Heavy Frigate. Skye doesn't have as much experience commanding larger vessels," Cobalt pointed out.

"That's right, I never heard you mention your older daughter before. Did something happen between you two?"

"You shouldn't open old wounds, Neriah."

"Ahem, Gil, you opened that can of worms yourself when you brought up my father earlier this afternoon, remember?"

Cobalt's expression soured a little. "Right," he admitted. "I forgot about that."

After a few more moments of silence he continued. "What happened is she fell for the wrong guy. I told her about it, she married him anyway, had a kid, found out what a jerk he was, and then blamed me for not trying harder to stop her sooner… or something dumb like that. We haven't spoken for ten years."

Solis stared in disbelief at her commanding officer. She had no idea of the troubles that existed in the Cobalt family. They had always had such a proud military history, that it never even occurred to her that they could have such problems.

"I'm sorry I asked. It was none of my business."

"Don't worry about it. You would have found out soon enough. I need to ask you to do me a favor. It is strictly voluntary."

Neriah sensed a potential nightmare coming on.

"I don't suspect that Melissa will act in any manner other than professional, but I think it would be better if she received the orders from you."

Neriah was taken aback. "Are you serious? You want me to be your go-between? Gil, isn't that just a little childish?"

"I said you could refuse. I'm a big boy. If you don't want to do it, I'm not going to order you to."

She hated being put on the spot. This was one of those situations where one thing was said, but another thing was meant. It infuriated her that he had this power over her when nobody else did. She let out a large sigh, just enough for her meaning to be conveyed. "Alright, I'll do it. I don't like it, but I'll do it."

"Thank you, Neriah."

Gil returned to staring out the viewport. Solis figured that the flight would be a non-speaking flight, so she reclined the seat and closed her eyes to sleep.

Chapter 4

Sorthac awoke in a haze. He tried to get up, but was held back by a wave of nausea. He resisted the immediate urge to stand and merely rolled over to face up instead. His eyes started to clear and he could make out the vague shape of Lieutenant Junior Grade Heather Martinez staring down at him intently. He blinked a couple of times trying to clear his vision.

"Are you alright sir?" She asked.

"My head hurts from the bump a pulse rifle deposited there and I have pain in my leg from a blast I received, but otherwise, I am undamaged." He suddenly became acutely aware of the pain from the rifle blast in his leg and winced a little. The young Lieutenant was obviously startled by the sudden movement, but she quickly regained her composure.

"Let me help you, sir." She grabbed some of his bulk and helped him into a sitting position. His vision was starting to clear. *Good*, he thought. *Hopefully I did not receive a concussion from the butt of the rifle striking my head.*

"Do we have any idea how many of them there are," he asked.

"I've been trying to keep track," said Petty Officer third class Wilson Barnes. "I've seen at least four, but there has to be more. They seem to be taking shifts watching us sir."

"Is there one of them watching us now?"

"Negative, sir. They seem to be handling some kind of minor emergency, but we were all gassed, so we have no idea what it may be."

Lt. Martinez nodded. "We can speak freely for the moment it appears, sir." She looked around. "Sir, I thought Commander Harrison was pulling bridge duty with you."

"She was. The last I saw her, she went to the head. She is not here?"

Lt. Martinez shook her head in the negative.

"Well, then Lieutenant, it looks like we may have an 'ace in the hole', provided our captors did not catch and kill her already."

"I hate falling asleep in tight spaces."

Lt. Commander Rachael Harrison tried to flex her still stiff limbs in the tight area. The security gas had knocked her unconscious, but since she was in the ventilator shaft, she was not discovered after she was knocked out. She kind of wished she had been discovered, because at least then she would know if Commander Sorthac was all right. But she didn't have time for that. She had to get to the security station and the weapons locker if her plan was going to work. First, she had to mask herself from the internal sensors, then she had to get into the weapons room and get a pulse rifle. At least she still had her personal sidearm, but it wasn't going to be enough against a group of armed terrorists. She needed some heavier hardware. The weapons locker on the hangar deck seemed like a good candidate as it was a large area that was difficult to guard with only a small force. She crawled another thirty feet and stopped. The marking on the wall read "Junction C34." *Only twelve decks and thirty more sections to go*, she thought.

Jason paced the bridge. He stopped briefly at the science console, then the weapons console. He checked and then rechecked the readings. He didn't like what he saw.

"They're not here. Where the hell are they?"

Samantha looked over at him. "Trust me, they'll be here. Have a little faith," she reassured him.

"I'm sorry. I just get a little jittery when things don't go exactly according to schedule. They are late and—" The proximity alarms started to wail. Outside the huge starship a marine troop transport materialized from hyperspace. The hailing signal appeared on the communications board.

"Commander, they are hailing us," Jerry notified.

"'Bout time. Open a channel."

"Commander, we are ready to begin transporting personnel over to your vessel to continue the plan. We await your signal." Came the husky voice of the marine

Captain.

"We're ready to receive you Captain. Come on over."

"Affirmative Commander."

Within moments, the transport shuttle had brought over the first wave of marines. One hundred fifty souls in all would be joining the rag-tag team of thieves aboard the starship *Moonhawk*. Thus fulfilling the minimum requirements to pilot the mega-ship.

Lt. Commander Harrison could see the first wave of troops come aboard from her vantage point in the vents above the hangar deck. *Shit*, she thought. *This complicates matters.* To make matters worse, the uniforms these soldiers were wearing had the markings of the Star Alliance Marine Corps on them. A man dressed like a Navy SEAL was ordering them into position. *What the hell is going on here*, she thought. The weapons locker was only five feet away from her, but one false move at this point would spell her doom, so she waited a little longer for the troops to clear out. When the coast was clear, she carefully opened the grating and climbed down.

She scurried over to the weapons locker keyed in the code and the lock slid easily open. *Hmm, there are perqs to being the Operations Officer*, she thought. She hefted out the bulky pulse rifle with practiced ease. She was a much more impressive package than her minuscule frame let on.   Good, the rifle was fully charged. She slung the weapon onto her shoulder and made for the grating again, only this time she wasn't so fortunate. A pulse blast ricocheted off the railing and she jumped back against the wall. She flopped down on her belly and drew her sidearm, took aim and fired at one of the assailants using the stunner setting. The man crumpled in a heap, unconscious. The other attacker fired a steady barrage of blanketing fire. She realized that if she stayed, she would be pinned. Seconds later, another marine showed up on the scene. It was only a matter of time.

Harrison rolled over and stood up sharply with the pulse rifle in hands fired some covering shots. The two marines scattered; soon two more joined them. *This is intolerable, and the odds aren't getting any better,* she lamented to herself. She fired two more shots and one of the other new arrivals took cover behind some zero-g crates. She only had seconds before they would be on top of her, so she had to do something quick. She scanned the territory and suddenly found her savior: two canisters of aviation fuel at the far side seventy-five feet away. Not close enough to kill them, but definitely enough to get their attention. She stood and took aim at the canister's release valve and took the shot. It was a miss! More blanketing fire drove her back behind the railing again. *Damn it all to hell, they're going to get me!* She stood once more and took aim. *Come on Rachael, you didn't win three awards for marksmanship shooting like this.* She squeezed the trigger.

The canister exploded in a brilliant flash sending

out a wave of fire across the hangar deck. The blast knocked the four marines against the bulkhead below Rachael and rendered them immediately and thoroughly unconscious. The other marines coming to their aid were stopped in their tracks at the threshold.

Rachael wasted no time. She ran through the doorway to her right and right down the corridor. She knew she didn't have much time before they tracked her down, so she ducked into one of the unoccupied crew quarters on that deck and shut the sliding doors. She disabled the locking mechanism so that nobody would be able to get in from the outside. She could hear the troops running past the outside of the door and she remained completely motionless in the darkness. When she couldn't hear the footfalls outside anymore, she slumped against the wall and let out a sigh of relief. *I see way too much action for my age,* she thought to herself. Now she was armed. The next goal would be rescuing the guards from the security division. But first, she decided to take a quick nap, not voluntarily, but her body was running on adrenaline so long that it just gave into the fatigue and she submitted to the oblivion of sleep right there in a heap on the deck.

Jason paced in front of the five singed marines. The look of disgust was plastered on his face.

"Tell me again how this mere slip of a girl managed to incapacitate all five of you *at once*," he demanded.

"Well, Commander, you see…"

"Shut the fuck up, Sergeant! It was a rhetorical question!" The marine lapsed into silence.

"What I really want to know, is how in the name of all that is holy did you two idiots let her fall through the cracks. I thought you reviewed the entire duty roster for who would be on board this ship during the graveyard watch."

"We did, Commander." It was Jerry who spoke up. "Sir, we checked it backwards and forwards, there was no mention of her in the duty roster for last night."

"Well, Master Chief, *obviously* she was added at the last minute."

"Sir, I might be able to shed some light on the situation," Samantha said.

"Well, don't keep us in suspense Lieutenant."

"Sir, Sergeant Gomez described a five-foot, four-inch maybe five-five lithe red-haired lieutenant commander in his report. I checked the database and came up with a match. She's Lt. Commander Rachael Harrison. She is the Operations Officer… and an ex-SEAL."

"Great. We have one of the people who knows every nook and cranny of this ship like the back of her hand, as well as our operating manual, running loose. Oh, and she took down five of our best men with a couple of well placed shots and a canister of fuel," Jason commented. His face was beet red. "I want this little—

thorn taken care of," he commanded. "Nobody travels alone, I don't want any unnecessary casualties. Oh, and people, remember, *she is not our enemy.* She simply has not been made to understand our goals. We are only borrowing the ship, but she probably doesn't see it that way. Don't forget that she could have killed all of you, but she didn't."

There was a quick round of 'yes sirs' and the contingent came to order.

"Dismissed."

The marines cleared the room and Sam drew closer to Jason to speak to him privately.

"So, what do we do now, sir?"

"Well, we continue on course. There isn't enough time to dilly-dally. Billions of lives are at stake, and we are their only hope. We need to stay focused." He looked around the room and then back at the younger Lieutenant. He clasped her shoulder and said in a reassuring voice: "This is just a temporary setback."

Captain Melissa Cobalt of the Heavy Cruiser *Galahad* swung around in the control chair.

"Commander Barker, as soon as the Admiral's shuttle is secured I want us to jump back to our pursuit course at flank speed."

"Yes sir," the commander responded.

The *Galahad* may not be a more powerful ship than the *Moonhawk*, but she did have superior speed, and that was something that she was counting on to be the deciding factor in the engagement that lay ahead. At least that stratagem seemed less complicated than having her father on board the ship. She wasn't truly loathe to see him, but after the way they had left things ten years ago, she wasn't sure how difficult it would be to mend fences.

Not that she was admitting that he had a right to meddle in her affairs, after all, she was younger then, and now she was ten years older. She was a seasoned veteran and a pretty damn good captain in her own right. She didn't need the 'Cobalt Legacy' following her around to make life grand.

"Captain, the Admiral's shuttle is secure in the hangar bay," Commander Barker intoned form the tactical station.

"Excellent. Helm, resume our pursuit course. Mr. Monahan, have Admiral Cobalt's team escorted to the tactical/situation room."

"Aye aye, Captain."

She stepped out of the chair and made her way to the motivator shaft. "Lieutenant Kresta, you have the conn," she said. The blond-haired female lieutenant nodded deferentially and moved to the center seat. As the doors to the motivator started to close, she heard the captain mutter to Commander Barker.

"Let's go meet our guests."

The hangar deck was alive with activity. Technicians were running everywhere securing cargo. Admiral Cobalt was the first to step down from the shuttle. He was immediately pushed aside by a series of techs carrying some fairly heavy gauge cable.

"Excuse me sir. We need to secure the shuttle for dimensional warp."

"Oh, let me get out of the way," he said apologetically.

"Admiral!"

Cobalt searched for the voice in the chaos. Across the hangar deck he could see Captain Ishido Kamazaki, Chief Engineer of the starship *Moonhawk* waving at him to join the group that had gathered. Cobalt and Solis quickly joined them. Gathered around Kamazaki were some of Cobalt's other senior staff members. He immediately saw the face of Commander Amy Ling, leader of the Blue Dragon's squadron. It made him feel more at ease about their chances of recovering the *Moonhawk* intact that either by choice or design, his best officers were present for the mission. He smiled quickly at them all.

"Well, now all we need is Dr. Lopez and Commander Ardenz, and we'll have a bona fide family reunion here," Cobalt joked.

"Actually, sir, Commander Ardenz and Dr. Lopez are in the science lab," Kamazaki said.

"I'm glad to see the whole team coming together."

"Sir, we should get off the hangar deck. They're preparing for a Warp," Ling pointed out.

"Captain Cobalt should be waiting for us in the situation room, sir."

"Let's go, then. I don't want to keep her waiting."

The situation room was tense. There was a display that covered the entire wall showing the sector they were currently traveling. A green triangle represented the *Galahad* and her two escorts, the destroyer *Ares*, and the corvette *Lafayette*. Further away on the map was a red glowing dot that represented the *Moonhawk* moving away at top cruising speed. Everyone was talking at once. The scene was reminiscent of the control tower a mere twelve hours before. The senior officers of the *Galahad* seemed embroiled in a debate with Dr. Heather Lopez and Chief Science Officer Jono Ardenz.

"Doctor, I cannot authorize continued research on a potentially lethal bio-agent to continue on board this ship," said Dr. Fatimah Wilson.

"Dr. Wilson, this bio-agent is only harmful to the bio-mimmetic seals on the shield generators. If we neutralize them, the shields will not be a hindrance to us and we can stop the *Moonhawk* without destroying her."

"I'm sorry, Dr. Lopez, but Dr. Wilson is right. The Alcar Accord of 2557 strictly prohibits the development of bio agents. *Regardless* of intended purpose," said *Galahad* security chief Alex Bowman.

"I'm afraid I'm going to have to agree with the commander there Doctor. Besides, payload delivery becomes a problem," Admiral Gilliad Cobalt stated as he strolled into the room.

"Admiral on deck!"

"As you were, people. Where is Captain Cobalt?"

"I'm right here," stated Captain Melissa Cobalt as she walked in with Commander Dennis Barker. She strode over to the head of the conference table and sat down in her customary place. Her body language confirmed for all that although *Admiral* Cobalt was in command of the mission, *she* was the captain of this vessel and all decisions were routed through her.

Commodore Solis ushered the crewmembers from the *Moonhawk* into corresponding positions around the table. Admiral Cobalt lingered until everyone was seated and noticed that the only seat left was the one on the extreme opposite end of the table from his estranged daughter. He sighed and took the chair. Commander Ardenz began the briefing.

"At this point, we still have no idea who is responsible for the theft of the *Moonhawk*. Naval counter-intelligence has some theories, but no real leads," he began. "Thanks to some quick action by Admiral Eubanks, the *Hornet* and the *Wasp* bought our tracking system enough time to trace the intended course the thieves appear to be taking."

He activated his electronic pointer and turned to the tactical display on the far wall. It swerved in closer to show the sector in more detail.

"We also know that they made a rendezvous of some kind in the Freemantle system, presumably because five is far too small of a crew to keep the ship operational for any length of time. We suspect that the perpetrators met up with some kind of marine transport to obtain the crew necessary to run the ship."

"Do we know where they are headed now, Commander? Commander Barker asked.

"Projected headings indicate that they are attempting to get to the Berali system," Ardenz responded.

"What the hell is in the Berali system," asked Commodore Solis.

"We're still waiting on the intelligence reports, sir."

She looked down at the table. Captain Cobalt didn't miss a beat.

"How long until we intercept?"

"Approximately fifty-seven hours, sir."

Gil looked expectantly at his first officer. She seemed lost in thought.

"Commodore Solis, do you have something you want to share with the group?" prodded Admiral Cobalt.

She looked up from the table, as if her mental train just derailed. "The Berali are embroiled in some kind of interplanetary war. It kind of resembles the Centauri War of 2196. I think that the race they are fighting with is known as the *'Empeewee'* or something like that."

" T h e *'Empiri'*, sir?" Commander Barker suggested.

"Yes, that's it exactly."

"How come this is the first time I have ever heard of these two races?" Admiral Cobalt asked.

"That is because they were only a minor footnote in the Two-Decades War, Admiral," Captain Kamazaki stated.

"Why would anyone be interested in a 'minor footnote', Captain?"

"Because," supplied Melissa Cobalt. "The Star Alliance has been trying to resolve the conflict between these two warring races for twenty-five years."

"Actually, Captain Cobalt, the war is over. It has been for over a year." Everyone turned sharply to look at Captain Kamazaki. "The Empiri inadvertently destroyed themselves when there was a chemical weapons malfunction during testing." Then he added cryptically: "They obviously weren't smart enough to do their testing away from their homeworld."

"But why did the war end? Surely their space forces were not diminished, Dr. Lopez said.

"The Empiri were a people that believed that a race without a homeworld was not worthy of survival. They committed mass suicide." The whole room was dead silent. Gil Cobalt spoke next.

    "If the war is over, and the Empiri are dead, what would anyone want with the Berali?"

Chapter 5

Sorthac continued to ignore his burned knee. The pain wasn't as sharp anymore; it was more like a dull ache at this point. He kept trying to consider escape routes, but he had come to the conclusion several hours ago that such an attempt would be futile. The new brig was engineered to be virtually escape-proof. Short of walking right through the electronic field in front of him or the captors miraculously setting them free, they weren't getting out of there any time soon. Lt. Heather Martinez, Petty Officer Barnes and the twenty or so security personnel seemed to be trying every angle of the escape option without much success. Even the various guards that were posted to check up on them seemed rather undisturbed by the fact that every panel that could be removed from the inside of the cell was now lying on the deck.

Truthfully, Sorthac was glad he was injured. If he had been at full capacity, the junior officer's morale and the morale of the crewmen in the cell would have degraded from his inactivity. Chotan did not waste time on frivolities, and a futile escape attempt from their own brig ranked at the top of that list. If the possibility of escape had actually existed, Sorthac would have been the first to try, injury or no. But as head of security, he knew the truth. Rather than spread an air of defeatism, he opted to stay quiet.

"Sir, were having no luck here. Any suggestions?"

"I'm formulating an attack plan even as we speak, Lieutenant," he lied.

"Yes sir. We'll keep trying, sir."

"I have faith in you, Mr. Martinez." She gave him a stiff smile. The hours of incarceration were starting to wear on her, but she looked determined not to go stir-crazy. Sorthac was just about to return to picking at the burned cloth of his khaki pants when the doors to the security division slid open. Sorthac craned his massive, scaly neck to get a better look at the new arrivals. A flicker of hope sprang up as he thought that it might be Lt. Commander Harrison, but it was quickly dashed as they came into view. It was that smug Jason fellow. Lt. Martinez saw him out of the corner of her eye and immediately lit up.

"Sir, I can't believe it, they actually sent you to rescue us!" She snapped him a quick formal salute. Sorthac shot her a look. He wasn't sure what he was witnessing.

"What are you doing, Lieutenant. These are our captors!"

"Impossible, sir. Don't you know who this is, sir?" Sorthac had to admit he was at a loss.

"No, I don't, Lieutenant. I only know him as 'Jason' if that is his real name."

"Oh, yes sir. It is. This is Lieutenant

Commander Jason Cobalt. And standing next to him is Lieutenant Samantha Wherlinger. This is SEAL Team Five, Sir!"

Sorthac stared in utter shock. To think that he was being held hostage by the Navy's elite had him flabbergasted.

"I'm afraid that the young lieutenant is correct about one thing. We are the members of SEAL Team Five. We also have with us the Second Platoon First Division Marine Force Recon with us to help. Were just not here to rescue you," he stated matter-of-factly.

"You have betrayed your country and your people, Commander. You will not get away with this," Sorthac warned. "In fact, they'll probably re-institute hanging just for you." Lt. Martinez looked absolutely crestfallen.

"And I suppose you think that by wearing the uniform of the Star Alliance Navy you're some kind of patriot, lizard man?" he sneered. "You have no idea what this is even about, but you are all ready to condemn me. If that ain't the pot calling the kettle black, I don't know what is." Sorthac considered his statement for a moment. Sorthac's words did seem a little bit hypocritical, given that the Chotan were once the mortal enemies of Humanity, but he decided not to give in.

"You have brought shame to your father's name," he fired back instead.

"Y'know, Commander, I'd love to tell you what

is going on here, but I'm afraid that will have to wait for another time."

"I can hardly wait."

"Oh, and he will never know, sir. No one will ever know. Not even you."

"What do you mean?"

Jason produced a vial of blue liquid. "Because of this," he said. "You have to understand, Commander, the marines and my team that joined this little expedition have careers and families. I didn't ask them to come along for the ride just to throw that all away. You seeing us was not part of the plan, but as a contingency, I had this little number whipped up. After we administer it to you, the next thing you will remember is waking up at Bethesda Naval Hospital when it is all over, and you will have no recollection of me, or my team."

Lt. Martinez jumped at him. "You worthless piece of crap!" But Sorthac used his considerable strength to wrap his arm around her waist and prevent her from clawing Jason's eyes out, as well as avoid the rifle butt that he knew would fall squarely on the back of her head if she had succeeded in getting off the bench.

"I'm not a bad person. I'm not doing this for me. Someday, you will understand. Someday, everyone will understand." And with that, he turned and walked out of the brig.

How to Steal a Starship

Rachael Harrison woke with a start. She sat upright in the darkened crew quarters she had located refuge in. She was stiff from sleeping on the deck, but she felt rested, like she had slept for years. She also felt sticky form the sweat that had dried on her. She looked around for a chrono. The timepiece read fourteen thirty-two. *Wow, I really conked out*, she thought. She stood up, stretched and caught a whiff of herself. *Aack*, she thought. *They won't have to use locators to find me. All they'll have to do is smell me out.* She looked around for the bathroom and walked in.

I'm safe for the moment, she thought. *If I'm quick, they won't detect me using the waterless shower.* She stripped off her uniform and placed it in the recycling unit to be processed and cleaned, thus revealing her tight little package. She undid the clasp that held her straight red hair together and let it fall around her shoulders and across breasts that were slightly more than handfuls. She looked at herself in the mirror above the sink inspecting every inch of her body for contusions, scrapes, bumps, and bruises, but found only some redness on her supple form where she received a flash burn from the fuel canister exploding. She had the formation of a six-pack on her stomach from constant exercise in the gym. She loved swimming and running. She trained with the SEAL's even after she left the organization because of the many missions where she flew as their pilot, and the regimen stayed with her. She wasn't exceptionally muscular, but she was definitely cut. Satisfied with her self-inspection, she stepped into the shower stall. The electro-magnetic waves were like magic fingers working every pore of her body. She always let out a little quiver when she took these showers, but she didn't have the luxury of time to take a bath, or a water shower.

When the cycle was complete she stepped out of the unit and grabbed her hair clip. This was one of those times she wished she were still on the complete SEAL regimen; her long hair was proving to be something of a hindrance to her at the moment. When she worked out with the SEAL's, her hair was almost completely shorn off. She shrugged her bare shoulders and retrieved her freshly cleaned uniform from the dispenser. Within a window of five minutes, she was back at one hundred percent. She grabbed the pulse rifle from the corner, checked her sidearm and cautiously opened the door. She poked her head out into the corridor and saw it was empty. *Lucky*, she thought. *They must have bigger fish to fry*.

She headed down the corridor slowly at first, then she picked up speed. At each junction she slowed a little to scout ahead and see if there were any guards approaching. She arrived at the main access ladder that ran parallel to the main motivator shaft and climbed inside. She stopped to figure out her next move.

What was it that Admiral Cobalt told me about the security systems onboard this ship, she wondered. She pondered the question for a moment. She was losing precious time but it came to her in a flash. *Of course*, she thought. *The Admiral told me that the security systems could be overridden from the captain's quarters.* It was a little secret that he had designed into the ship when it was being built. She began the steady twenty-deck climb up the ladder to the officer's living quarters. Suddenly she heard voices approaching and stopped dead in her tracks.

"I don't care what it takes, I want you to catch her. I know this 'little girl' you keep referring to and I can tell you, she's no kid."

"Jerry, I can't believe you're afraid of this kid."

He stopped for a second. "Sam, she's not just a kid. I remember her, but the last time I saw her, she was a Chief Warrant Officer three and she was being awarded the Medal of Honor for saving our whole team. She knows the way we do things backwards and forwards. And she has a lot of experience in combat situations for her age."

Like you would know, Rachael thought with mild irritation.

"Mark my words. You guys underestimate this little tart, and you're gonna get burned," he warned. They continued down the corridor in silence. Rachael remained completely still for a few extra moments before she was convinced they were gone and then she resumed her climb.

It seemed like hours had passed, but Rachael finally reached her destination. With one hand she held the ladder, with the other hand she stuck her weapon around the corner and peeked out. The coast seemed clear. She slipped into the corridor and made her way down the length of the first corridor. It forked after about thirty feet and then she stopped. Which way to go? She wasn't entirely sure which fork to take, she had only been to the captain's quarters once, and that was only to deliver a message. She was completely at a loss for which direction. *The road less taken,* she thought ironically. The decision was made for her when she heard voices from the other corridor. She quickly dropped into one of the doorway's to avoid being seen.

"Sergeant, I want her found. We cannot save the Berali if we are dodging friendly fire on board this ship."

"Sir, we have searched the entire ship, but it is more massive than our small numbers can search. The deck plan is enough for over fourteen city blocks spread out a mile long and over a quarter-mile wide. Even with internal sensors, we're not on some popular science fiction show, sir. I can't just 'beam' troops to her location."

"That's an interesting comment, Sergeant. Tell Major Braxton that I share his concern that we don't have enough personnel, but considering the risk of the operation, I wanted to minimize exposure."

Rachael tried to get a good look at the man who was obviously higher ranked. He looked oddly familiar to her. Perhaps it was his blue eyes and the intensity of his gaze, but he reminded her of someone. She just couldn't place who it was. She burned the image of his face into her memory for future reference and prepared to move out as soon as they were out of range.

The remaining stretch of corridor was silent as she made her way to Admiral Cobalt's quarters. She felt like she had backtracked at least a dozen times before she finally came to the door with his name on the plate. She keyed in the security code and the door slid open. *At least they didn't change the master door codes,* she thought.

As she entered the Admiral's quarters she couldn't help but feel that this was a tremendous violation of the Admiral's privacy. She had a considerable amount of respect for the revered admiral. She also looked up to him as a role model, and he was like an uncle to her.

She crossed into the middle of the main room. The captain's quarters were like a palace to the young Lt. Commander, but then again, on a ship this size, the senior officers could afford the luxury of spacious quarters. *Hell*, she though. *My own quarters are bigger than my first apartment.*

There was an odd looking nightstand on the opposite side of the Admiral's bed. It looked almost like a decorative crate that was built into the floor. *It must be there,* she thought. She reached around the side of the peculiar piece of furniture to feel for a switch and that was when the object caught her eye. It was an old style photograph inside an oak frame. In it she could see the admiral's family. She saw Admiral (Then Captain in the photo) Cobalt looking smart in his dress whites and standing to his left was a Lieutenant Commander he imagined to be his deceased wife Sarah. To her left was a young auburn haired girl with a cane. Rachael assumed that was his youngest daughter Skye. To the right of Cobalt was a young woman in a lieutenant's uniform. She guessed that was his oldest child, Melissa. She had heard the admiral mention his family many times during staff meetings. He always seemed proud of his daughters even though he had mentioned that he and Melissa rarely spoke anymore. But there was on other figure in the picture. It was a very green looking Ensign who looked like a much younger version of the admiral. A young man who looked almost exactly like the man she just saw in the corridor mere moments ago.

"Oh my God," she said out loud.

She quickly turned her attention back to the table. She had a renewed sense of urgency. Everything came into focus now. Jason Cobalt was his name. He was a member of SEAL Team Five when she rescued them from the ambush on Velinius Three; the very mission she was awarded the Medal of Honor for. Her actions saved the entire eleven-man team. Now she had a small pang of regret that she saved this particular member, but how could she have known this would happen?

She felt a notch in the back of the table and

pressed it with her finger. The top of the table slid back and a command interface rose up from inside. She activated the console and began to input the security codes.

Chapter 6

The Heavy Frigate *Galahad* sped through space on her pursuit of the starship *Moonhawk*, her escorts following shortly after. On the bridge the tension was thick. Everyone was literally on the edge of their seat (those who had seats). Even the spaceman at the helm was clenching the wheel.

"Captain, we're gaining on them. Entering the range of our long range radar, sir."

"Put the tactical display on the holo-viewer, Ensign."

"Aye, Captain."

The schematic appeared on the tri-dimensional display in translucent relief. A wireframe image of the *Moonhawk* was shown moving away from them at top speed, but the distance seemed to be closing slightly between them.

"Time to intercept?"

"If we continue at one hundred percent power, we will catch them in approximately nine hours, twenty-seven minutes."

"How long until they reach Belaria, Ensign," asked Commander Barker.

"At their present speed, they will reach Belaria in eight hours, forty-three minutes, sir," the Ensign responded.

Captain Cobalt opened her mouth to issue an order, but stopped for a moment, then looked at her father and his first officer.

"What do you think, Admiral?"

Solis stepped forward and cleared her throat. "I think the admiral thinks…"

"I'm sorry, Commodore, but with all due respect, I asked the *Admiral* for his opinion, as he is the mission commander."

The remark was so insubordinate; it stopped all activity on the bridge. Solis was outraged. She stepped closer to Melissa Cobalt so that she was almost toe-to-toe with her. Captain Cobalt didn't even flinch. She just stared back at Solis with dead eyes.

"Now you listen here, Captain, you have no right —" but Admiral Cobalt placed his hand on her shoulder ever so gently.

"Take it easy there sailor. I'll handle this. This has been a long time in coming," and then he added, "but thanks for trying." She realized that he wasn't about to let his daughter and his best friend come to blows. The Admiral walked to the stairwell leading to the conning tower and gestured for Melissa to follow.

"Shall we, Captain?"

She took a sharp inward breath, held it for a moment and moved to follow him to the tower. They climbed the stairs in silence, neither one looking at the other. When they reached the top Admiral Cobalt stood aside so his daughter could enter the tower first. He followed after she was inside and closed the door behind them. She folded her arms as if she were bracing herself for a barrage. Gil Cobalt just stared at her. After a moment he spoke, calmly.

"Y'know, I'm still trying to figure out where we went wrong, Melissa."

"*We*, didn't go wrong sir. *You* did." He gave her a perplexed look.

"I'm sorry, Melissa, but since when is a father telling his daughter that she's making a mistake going wrong?"

"That's just it, you're always meddling!"

"Well, little missy, I have news for you: That's what parents do! We meddle. We get in the way and take the hit for you doing something stupid. *We protect!*"

"Ha! You never protected anyone. Not even mother!"

The rage boiled over in Cobalt and he slapped her across the face, hard. She staggered back a little, shocked at the assault.

"Striking a fellow officer is a court martial offense, sir!" She yelled, her eyes on fire.

"So, report me to the Judge Advocate General. It's your word against mine. Besides, I didn't strike a fellow officer. I was a father slapping some sense into his petulant daughter. You have absolutely no right to speak about me that way. I did everything short of die in her place, and still I couldn't save your mother. Not a day goes by without me wishing I had died in her place, if only I could have saved her. And I never abandoned you, or Skye, or Jason."

"Your career was always more important," she sniffed.

"Drop the wounded little girl act, Melissa. You are too strong for that kind of crap, and you don't do it very well. You were always the independent one. You never needed anybody. I know, I tried to be there for you. Truth is, Melissa, I was there for you more than you were there for yourself. I got tired of being pushed away, so I gave up trying. If you want to keep acting like I'm dead, then as far as I'm concerned, I don't have a daughter anymore, except Skye."

She looked down at the deck. Admiral Cobalt started to leave and put his hand on the door latch.

"Wait," she said.

"What is it," he asked.

"I'm sorry for the things I said. I was angry with you ten years ago, but the truth is that you're right. About Harvey and about me. I have always pushed people away. And he was a jerk. I was always an overachiever and I felt I didn't need help from anybody, and that's what I needed more than anything else. I've had nobody to turn to for years, and I keep my own counsel, even now."

Gil's expression softened as he spoke. "Melissa, that's not true. You *always* had someone to turn to. *Me*."

"You would have helped me, even after all of the hurtful things we said to each other all those years ago," she asked.

He smiled at her. "Melissa, sweetheart, just because we said some things back in the day, doesn't mean that I stop being your father and you stop being my daughter. I just wish you had said you needed help."

"I guess I'm a day late and a dollar short, it seems daddy."

"Hey, watch that daddy stuff. If we start getting misty in here, your crew might talk," he said slyly.

"*My* crew? Talk? What about *your* crew," she laughed.

"My crew already talks. I'm not worried about them." They both laughed and hugged for the first time in ten years. Gil Cobalt didn't want to let go. He let go of her once, and she almost never returned. He vowed never to let his family split like that again.

"Hey, I think our crews are waiting for a decision, dad."

"Yeah, I think so. What do you think? We're already running at one hundred percent. If we push it a little, we might be able to stop them from doing real damage."

"But, if we run at one hundred ten percent or even one twenty, we could lose half the ship," she protested.

"Don't worry about that. Let Ishido Kamazaki worry about that. He's gotten the *Moonhawk* to run far beyond factory specs, and I'm the one who designed her."

She smiled and nodded. "Then it's settled. One twenty it is." She felt the sting in the side of her face where Admiral Cobalt slapped her. "Ow, does it show?" She pointed to the spot on her face.

She had a bright red mark where he slapped her. "Er, no. It doesn't seem to be noticeable," he lied.

"I'll say I slipped."

"I'm sure they'll believe that…" he said sarcastically.

"Well, after the way I shot my mouth off, they probably expected you to cuff me one," she said.

"Speaking of shooting your mouth off, do not speak to Neriah that way again. She's your superior officer," he said in a scolding manner.

"Oh, when did she become 'Neriah' instead of 'Commodore Solis,' hmmm?"

"That is none of your business."

"Well, she's only five years older than me. You're old enough to be her father," she joked.

"Yeah, I'm old enough to be *your* father. Imagine *that.*"

She gave him a sideways glance, but her expression didn't sour. Gil was glad that they had buried the hatchet so quickly, it only lent credence to his theory that their feud was over trivialities, but he regretted hitting his daughter. He had never struck any of his children, ever. The comment she directed at him about not trying to protect Sarah, his wife, hit a little too close to home. He still wondered to that day whether he had done everything possible to save her.

The two of them left the conning tower and returned to the bridge. Everyone was silent. She strode over to the helm. The ensign at the wheel stared openly at the red welt on the left side of her face. She noticed it and redirected his attention.

"Do you find something interesting there, Mr. Ayers?"

"No, sir!"

"Good. Run us at one twenty."

"Y-Yes sir." Kamazaki left the bridge obviously bound for engineering muttering something about how 'they're gonna need him.' Gil Cobalt smiled knowingly. He sidled up to Solis. She looked at him with mild irritation. "Did you strike her?" she whispered.

"Friendly persuasion," he whispered back. He saw the look in her eye and added: "I'm just kidding. That's from an unrelated topic. Strictly father-daughter."

She obviously didn't like that answer any better, but she accepted it. The ship lurched a little, but took off at twenty percent above factory tolerances.

The watch on the bridge was uneventful. Sam was getting bored. For the last two days since breaking away from the two pursuing vessels in Earth orbit, they had seen neither hide nor hair of the Star Alliance Navy coming after them. She was a little disappointed that they hadn't. She always enjoyed a good challenge. Sitting at the helm of a starship on a straight course and not being shot at was not her idea of 'challenging.' She was annoyed that the Navy hadn't obliged her yet. Her annoyance must have been chiseled into her face, because Jerry started to engage her in conversation.

"Y'know, we are doing the right thing," he said.

She looked at him quizzically. "Huh?"

"That look on your face. You looked kind of bent out of shape, like we made the wrong choice."

"Jerry, I'm not bent out of shape about that. Saving billions of lives is not a mistake. I'm just a little pissed that the Navy hasn't sent up much resistance to our plans."

Jerry considered the sentiment for a moment. "You know, I remember this one mission I was on early in my career…"

"Oh, God, Jerry. Not another one of your stories! How many of those do I have to hear?"

Jerry continued with the story, ignoring the complaints of his younger associate. "As I was about to say, I was on a intel gathering mission in the Kkhakris system on the far side of Crysalian space. We were completely invisible. They had no idea we were even there and I remember wishing to myself that they did, because I wanted to take a shot at them really bad. I had never even seen a Crysalian before, but I was trained to know they were the enemy. When you are young, you cling to these notions of black-and-white." He paused to take a deep breath before continuing.

"We were about to pack it out with our mission accomplished when we spotted a foot patrol. The commanding officer motioned for all of us to lay low and stay out of sight. He figured if they weren't scanning for us, they wouldn't find us. The guards walked up and down. The first time I laid eyes on one I got jumpy. My hands clenched around the pulse rifle that much tighter. He started moving closer to the team. I knew he couldn't see me, but I made eye contact, so in my mind he had seen us. The CO told us to stay put. We were gonna try and get out with as little noise as possible, but my mind was locked into that notion that he was heading straight for me. I gave the signal that I had been spotted, and I jumped out of my hiding place and gunned the guard down. The other guard came running at us, his weapon blazing. I took him out too, but a glancing shot hit me in the shoulder and another hit one of my buddies. This alerted the other guards and all of a sudden, we had the whole Goddamned Crysalian army on top of us. It was a hell of a fight; we lost three more men before we got to the shuttle. Of the twelve man team, eight of us made it back to the shuttle in basically one piece, some had some pretty serious plasma rifle burns, though. When we got back, they gave me a medal and said that I saved the remaining team members from certain death. If only they had known the truth."

Samantha looked at him for moment. She still looked irritated, but now it appeared that it was directed at him. "What the hell was that? Is that it? So you panicked way back in your youth. Every rookie makes dumb mistakes, even mistakes that get someone killed, or a lot of someone's. You saved the rest of the team. That has to count for something. Besides, there is no way you could have known whether or not he did see you, but one thing is for sure, if he had gotten any closer you would all have been dead and you and I wouldn't be having this ridiculous conversation."

His cheeks were red with frustration. "The point, you dolt, is that you should be careful what you wish for or you may get it. If I hadn't wished for more action, we might have avoided the whole mess!"

She laughed out loud, the unpleasant ridiculing kind of laugh. "You actually think that because you wanted more action, you got it? Oh, Jerry, that's rich! To think for even one second that you have control over cosmic events like that is the most self absorbed—" But she never finished the sentence.

The ship lurched suddenly as the ion turrets took out her shields on the port side aft of the ship. Samantha and Jerry were thrown against their consoles.

"What the hell was that?" Jerry demanded.

"I'm reading three ships. A *Manasas* Class Heavy Frigate, a *Ares* class 'tin-can' and a *Albright*

Class Corvette just dropped out of hyperspace!"

"Ma'am," said one of the marines at the tactical station. "Our port side aft shields are gone. That volley took 'em out ma'am!"

"Battlestations!"

"What now," Jason Cobalt demanded.

"Sounds like Ion turret fire, sir," the sergeant said.

"We had better get to the bridge, quickly!"

The two men broke out in a dead run to the motivator shaft that led to the bridge and jumped inside the waiting car.

Lt. Commander Rachael Harrison felt the jolt and grabbed the console in front of her. The rocking lasted for a few seconds. *Must have hit us full force,* she thought. *If I know Admiral Cobalt correctly, he probably thought that would be necessary to get the attention of a ship like this one.*

She checked the sensor readout in front of her. *Hmmm, a Manasas Class ship. Not bad,* she thought. If she didn't act quickly there would be a battle and as impressive as the armaments of the *Manasas* Class were, they were no match for the *Moonhawk*. Any battle with those odds would go poorly for the heavy frigate. She decided to step up her attempts to circumvent the ship's security system. With mere moments left, any decision she made could mean life and death.

"Direct hit Captain! They're slowing down," reported the Ensign at the helm.

"Keep your fire path tight, Mr. Arless. We don't want them to be able to react. Target main shield junction points Alpha and Baker so we can disable their weapon systems."

They had been lucky Captain Melissa Cobalt thought to herself. With a little more luck they could disable the larger ship's shields and board her. She looked over at her father and realized he looked pensive. *Must be the fact that he has to stand here on the bridge and do nothing,* she thought. "Fire battery two," she ordered.

"Direct hit to grid Baker Seven, sir."

"Captain, a suggestion."

Captain Cobalt looked again in the direction of her father. "Yes, sir?"

"There is a distinct possibility that they are toying with us. We've been lucky so far. I would suggest a less aggressive 'hit-and-run' tactic as it would be less taxing on *our* resources while forcing them to commit more of theirs."

"Noted, Admiral. Mr. Arless, continue the attack."

Stupid! He thought. Maybe they would get lucky again and the thieves didn't have full command of the resources available to them onboard the *Moonhawk.*

Cobalt couldn't believe that she was reacting this way. *I guess it will take a lot more than just a smack in the face and a few tender moments to mend fences between us,* he thought bitterly. "Just try not to blow my damn ship completely to bits until we have to, Captain!"

Jason Cobalt arrived at the bridge of the *Moonhawk* in time to be thrown to the deck by another volley of ion fire from the attacking starships. He picked himself up off the floor with haste and moved to the helm.

"Give me a status report," he demanded.

"They took out our port side aft shields, sir. We're taking evasive maneuvers, but they keep pressing the attack, Commander."

"Then why run. We could cripple them without breaking a sweat or killing a single person. Hard about, Lieutenant Wherlinger." The humungous starship slowed and began a sharp turn to face the attacking vessels. "Sergeant Pearson, target the main drive pods of the destroyer with our torpedoes. One half power please."

"Aye sir. Obtaining shooting solution. Ready to fire, sir."

"Fire."

The torpedoes flew out of the tubes on the bow of the Dreadnought and struck the engine pods of the destroyer. Their engine pods exploded brilliantly and the ship spiraled. Without engines the ship had no flight controls. It continued spinning in space. The Corvette slid around the massive starship and continued its barrage. Meanwhile the *Galahad* swung around and continued its attack.

"The destroyer is dead in space, no crew casualties, but her engines were completely destroyed, sir. She's on battery power only."

"Excellent work, Sergeant. Now target the Corvette."

"Shooting solution acquired, sir."

"Take 'em out of commission, Sergeant."

This time the smaller turrets along the hull of the Moonhawk opened up and sent a rain of fire toward the tiny warship. Several of the beams struck the minuscule vessel's shields before they sputtered out of existence. A second volley of cover fire sprang forth from the Moonhawk's hull emplacements and stuck the small ship's engine compartment. The engines appeared to struggle for a moment before the main thrusters gave up the ghost. The ship simply drifted helplessly. The only ship left was the *Galahad*.

"Corvette is out of commission, Commander."

"Get me a shooting solution on the Frigate, Sergeant."

"Shooting solution imminent, sir."

The targeting computer took a few moments to lock on to the Galahad. Jason had to give the helm officer of the smaller ship credit. His erratic maneuvering was making it difficult to lock on, but it was only a matter of time before…

"Shooting solution acquired, sir."

"Prepare to fire."

Harrison keyed the final sequence into the console. It took her several hours to hack into the ships central computer. *I need to brush up on my hacking skills, I used to be faster with this stuff*, she thought.

The tactical display came up. *Oh, no*, she thought. *They took out the other two ships!* There was no time left, it was now or never. She saw the shooting solution on the *Galahad* and keyed in the sequence that would disable the pulse torpedoes.

"Ready to fire, sir."

"Fire."

Only this time there was no reaction. The frigate kept coming, firing energy bolts with each pass.

"What the hell happened, Sergeant? I gave the order, fire the damn torpedoes already," Jason Cobalt ordered.

"Commander, this isn't my doing. Someone has overridden the security protocols. I don't have weapon control anymore."

Cobalt moved quickly to the science station. "Transfer computer control to this console, Lt. Wherlinger."

"You have it, Commander."

Jason Cobalt worked the controls furiously. He

finally saw the reason for the problems. "Lt. Wherlinger, break off our attack. We have a bigger problem than that frigate. I need your code hacking skills over here. Hand the helm over to Chief Maxwell."

She handed the helm to Jerry and made her way quickly to the science console. She looked over Jason's shoulder and immediately saw the problem.

"It looks like someone has overridden command and control systems. They have taken main tachyon cannons and torpedo launch systems offline, but most of the other systems are intact. Let me reroute control of these systems now." Her hands flew over the console at lightning speed, inserting lines of code and blocking commands from the override station. After a few minutes that stretched like hours she looked up.

"Sir, I stopped whoever was overriding systems, but the main tachyon cannons are still off-line. We still have helm control, shields, and the torpedo tubes."

"But we can't fend off our friends out there?"

"Pretty much, sir."

"Where are they?"

"Sir, the override codes were input by Lt. Commander Rachael Harrison on the Officer's Quarters level one. The Captain's quarters."

He turned to the helm station. "Jerry, take a security detail down to the officer's quarters level and get that girl, NOW!"

Rachael Harrison knew better than to stay put.

Whoever these people had, they were far better hacker's than she was. All of her attempts to further sabotage the system met with 'access denied' warnings. It was pretty good hacking indeed, since this station had the command codes to override any station on the ship.

She grabbed her pulse rifle and headed for the door. She ran out into the corridor. The security level was one floor down. If she could get there, she could free her comrades and even the odds a little.

She turned down the next corridor toward the motivator shaft. "What have I got to lose at this point," she asked out loud, and leapt into the motivator car.

"What do you mean, their weapons are offline?"

"I mean that the energy signature from the *Moonhawk* indicates that their weapons have been powered down, Captain," the ensign responded.

"Captain, the *Moonhawk* is turning away form us. They are resuming their course, sir."

Through the viewport they could see the massive bulk of the *Moonhawk* turning away from them on a retreat course.

"Follow them, Ensign Monahan. Don't let them get away!" She turned toward Admirals Cobalt and Solis. "Sirs, what the hell was that?"

"I suspect that we have help on the inside," Said Neriah Solis unable to hide her smile.

"You see, Melissa, there was a full security contingent on board the Moonhawk while she was dry-docked.   I suspect that Commander Sorthac is a bit more resourceful than we all gave him credit for.   He must have engineered some kind of escape and is attempting to reclaim the ship even as we speak."

Chapter 7

Harrison was amazed at how many shots flew past her head without making contact. Truth be told, she was never a big fan of firefights, but she was finding herself in more than her fair share these days. "Yeah, I'll become the Ops officer. Nobody will shoot at me there," she said dryly. Only twenty more feet and she would be in the security division. Twenty feet and it seemed like sixty armed guards. She poked her head around the corner again and took another shot. This one connected and the guard went down. Actually, there was only three guards left. She took a quick inventory of the weapons on hand. Her pulse rifle's energy pack was spent and she had two service issues left. Her own, and the one she boosted from the admiral's quarters. She figured he wouldn't mind under the circumstances.

Another two shots hit the bulkhead near her shoulder. She readied the weapons in each hand. Her plan wasn't the greatest, but she was running out of time again, and her options were extremely limited. She inhaled a deep breath and swung out into the corridor, pistols blazing. The two guards reacted, surprised. The guard on the left tried to take aim, but when he stood to shoot he was struck squarely in the chest by a stun blast form Rachael's pistol. She ran forward and let out a yell. The other guard tried to aim, but he didn't get the chance. The shot went wild and Harrison leveled her own weapon on him and squeezed the trigger. The guard slumped to the floor unconscious.

She stepped over the body of the fallen guard and entered the security division. Lt. Martinez was the first on her feet.

"Commander Harrison, I can't believe it!"

"Your faith in me is overwhelming, Lieutenant."

Sorthac got to his feet with some effort. "It is about time you got here. I suspected that you had been apprehended somehow."

"Wow, Commander," she said. "If I knew that I was going to get this warm of a reception, I would have simply turned myself in. This hardly seems worth the effort." She placed her hands on her hips and stared directly at Sorthac. After a few moments he muttered "thanks."

"You're welcome, sir," she smiled and then tossed him a pistol. "Can you walk?"

Sorthac tested his bad leg and suppressed the grunt as he applied weight. As far as Sorthac was concerned, pain was something to be managed, not acknowledged. He stood firmly on his leg. Alarm bells were going off in his head, but using his carefully crafted discipline, he silenced them one by one.

"I'm ready. Let's go."

Lt. Martinez and several of the other crew members that were held captive picked up the rifles dropped by the three guards Harrison felled in the corridor. They dragged the unconscious soldiers inside the cell, activated the barrier and followed her and Sorthac out of the security division.

"What is happening?"

"Sir, the prisoners have escaped!"

"All decks, security alert!" But it was too late. The banging at the doors to the bridge made Jason turn with a start. "Quick, seal the doors!" But again it was too late. The doors blew inward and the crew scattered, rifles blazing. Sam went down first; she slumped against the helm and slid to the floor. Jerry tried a blitz attack, but was quickly cut down by an eagle-eyed shot from Harrison. The marines tried to regroup and cut the *Moonhawk* security officers from the escape routes. Lt. Martinez came around to the security station and took aim at Jason.

"Alright you assholes, drop it, or I drop him." She waved the weapon menacingly so that the marines could see the power indicator. It was set to full power and it was aimed directly at his head. The guards put their rifles down on the consoles slowly and backed away.

"What are you doing? Stun her already! If you don't obey my orders, billions will die!"

Sorthac had heard just about enough of that. "Oh, shut up, cretin." And with that he slugged Jason Cobalt in the side of his temple flooring him instantly. Lt. Martinez waved the weapon around again.

"Anybody else want a piece of this?" She asked.

A marine corporal spoke up. "No, ma'am. We didn't sign on so anybody got killed. We was just coming along to help save this planet, y'see, ma'am."

Lt. Commander Harrison stuck her finger in her ear and twisted it around, like she was having trouble hearing and needed to clean the space. "I'm sorry, I have to have my hearing checked, Corporal. What did you just say?"

The corporal gulped. "I said we was just trying to save this planet the Commander was tellin' us about, ma'am. Nobody was supposed to get hurt."

"Humph," Sorthac scoffed. "That's a good one marine. I'll have to remember that one at your court martial."

Suddenly it seemed like half a brigade of marines showed up at the door.

"Freeze!"

"Drop your weapons!"

Sorthac leveled his own weapon at the fallen form of Jason Cobalt. "No, gentlemen, I think it is you who will be dropping their weapons this evening." There was a stalemate. Then Sorthac heard another voice.

"Holster your weapons boys. The operation's been flushed."

The marines in the front hesitated as the looked around. There was a tense moment where Sorthac suspected he might have to do something drastic.

Instead, the apprehensive guards lowered their rifles. The crowd of gathered marines parted to let someone through. A marine major came forward. He stopped in front of Sorthac, came to attention and snapped off a formal salute. Sorthac looked a bit uncomfortable, unsure how to react.

"Major Francis Braxton, Commander. Second Division Force Recon Platoon. We're on an authorized mission and I think you have my CO on the floor."

"Major, what the hell is going on here," Sorthac demanded.

"I think the commander could explain that a little better than I, sir."

Jason Cobalt started groaning. "Whoa, someone get the license number of the shuttle that hit me." He tried to sit up. The *Moonhawk* security officer's weapons were all on him again.

"Commander Sorthac, I really don't think that is necessary, sir," Major Braxton said. "Believe it or not, we're on the same side in this one, even if you don't know it yet."

Sorthac stopped short. "What do you mean?"

"It's true, sir," Jason said. "You see, sir…"

"Hold it a second," Rachael interrupted. "Aren't we forgetting about that frigate that was chasing us not long ago?"

Everyone looked at one another, realizing the sudden lapse in attention.

"Tactical display!" Sorthac ordered.

How to Steal a Starship

The holo viewer came to life and showed the Heavy Frigate *Galahad* bearing down on them. Her weapons laced into the Moonhawk's shields again.

One of the shield displays on the defense station fluttered and disappeared.

"We lost one of our starboard shields!"

"Evasive maneuvers, Mister Harrison, NOW!" Sorthac ordered.

"Aye, sir," Harrison jumped on the wheel with practiced skill, but she started to struggle a little. "Commander, helm control is sluggish, they must have damaged one of our spatial rudders, sir!"

"Can you turn the damaged section away from their weapons?"

"I'll do my best, sir!"

"You better do more than just your best, Mister!"

"Aye, sir," she managed through gritted teeth.

"Lt. Martinez, open a channel to the *Galahad*! Let them know we have retaken the ship!"

Lt. Martinez worked the controls at the communications station furiously. After a few moments without a response, Sorthac lost his patience.

"How about sometime before we are dusted by one of our own, Lieutenant?"

"I'm trying sir, but communications aren't responding. I can't get a clear channel, sir," she responded.

Another volley rocked the massive ship.

"Damage to starboard shield three."

79

Still holding his head where Sorthac cuffed him, Lt. Commander Jason Cobalt struggled to the tactical station and checked the readouts.

"Commander, I know why they can't hear us. They are running their engine core at one twenty. The radiation from its exhaust is preventing us from transmitting a clear signal."

Sorthac looked at him skeptically. "And how can I trust this information you are giving me, Commander?"

"Sir, now is not the time for deception. Check the readouts for yourself."

Sorthac thought for a second. "No, that won't be necessary."

Lt. Wherlinger was still in a haze from the stun blast when she spoke. "Ironic that we have the most powerful ship in the Navy's arsenal and we're gonna get blown to bits by a Heavy Frigate." She slumped into the nearest chair to nurse her stun hangover.

Sorthac considered that thought for a moment. "Mister Harrison, release the security lockout on the main cannons. Lt. Martinez, bring our main tachyon cannons to twenty-five percent power, wide dispersal." Harrison and Martinez looked at him skeptically. "Trust me," he added.

"Aye sir," Harrison smiled.

She keyed in the command codes and released the lockout on the weapon systems. Lt. Martinez readied the tachyon cannons for wide dispersal.

"Weapons ready commander."

"What are you going to do Commander?" Jason asked.

"If we fire a wide dispersal blast near their engine exhaust it will ignite the gasses and cause them reduce speed to avoid overloading their engine core. Then we'll be able to get a signal through to them... at least that's the theory."

"And what happens if they don't?" he asked.

"Then, they'll most likely blow up."

"This is a fantastic plan, Commander. Y'know, my original plan didn't involve the harming of a SINGLE person. Congratulations."

"I'm sorry, am I going to be facing the court martial, or are you?"

"STOP IT, BOTH OF YOU!"

Sorthac and Jason both looked at the helm where the outburst came from. Harrison's eyes were blazing.

"We're about to be blown to bits by one of our own and all you guys can do is fight!" Another volley rocked the ship. Rachael pushed the strands of hair that popped loose from her clasp out of her face. Sorthac and Jason looked at each other.

"Y'know, Commander, she's right."

"I make it a habit not to dispute her very often."

"It's a long shot Commander, but I like bad odds better than no odds."

"Fire the cannon, Lt. Martinez."

The *Moonhawk* turned slowly toward the aft

while continuing its original momentum through the subspace ether. A wide beam shot forth from the gigantic weapon of mass destruction and it lanced across the space between the two ships. The beam struck the ionized plasma exhaust behind the *Galahad* and it exploded in a brilliant flash of light. For a moment it appeared as though the Heavy Frigate were attempting to outrun the blast, but any further effort to run would only lend fuel to the fire. The ship slowed abruptly as the wave of fire enveloped its shields and proceeded after the *Moonhawk*. Everyone on the bridge of the *Moonhawk* stared in utter disbelief as the wave of fire drew closer.

"Brace for impact!" Sorthac yelled.

The ring of fire overtook the Battleship within seconds. The ship shook violently. Alarms went off everywhere as what was left of the shields attempted to absorb the explosion. The feedback form the pulse wave caused circuitry to explode in a shower of sparks. The lights dimmed and changed to the blue that indicated that they were now on battery power.

"Turn us into the wave!" Jason yelled over the din.

"Aye-aye," Harrison yelled from the helm. She struggled with the wheel, but the strain was obvious on her face as the force feedback from the electronic rudder resisted the turn. She simply did not have the brute strength to force the already sluggish helm controls to bend to her will. Sorthac didn't hesitate for a second as he jumped in and grabbed the wheel with Lt. Commander Harrison. They both screamed in unison.

"Yeeeeeeeeeaaaaaaagh!"

Finally, the gigantic ship bent to their combined wills and answered the helm. The ship took a steep climb to ride the top of the energy wave as the shields took a terrible beating. Harrison counted on Sorthac's incredible strength to hold the wheel as she reached for the throttle and pulled back to reduce power. The ship began to lose velocity and the vibrating abated little by little. Finally the ship came to a dead halt. Nobody dared move for an eternity.

Jerry was already at the communications station. "Sir's, the *Galahad* is signaling us!"

Sorthac strode over to the station. He pushed the Master Chief away form the console and brought up the communiqué on the viewpanel. Captain Melissa Cobalt's face appeared on the monitor. Her expression was absolutely livid. Sorthac could see Admiral Cobalt looking concerned in the background.

"What the hell is going on, Commander," she demanded.

"We have managed to regain control of the ship, Captain. I am attempting to ascertain precisely what is going on here. Please stand by." Captain Cobalt looked as though she wanted to object, but Sorthac cut off the channel before she could actually say anything.

"Alright, Mr. Cobalt. You have precisely five minutes to convince me that I shouldn't throw you out the nearest airlock as opposed to simply letting you stand trial for 'misappropriating' government equipment."

"If my plan had worked, we would have saved billions of people, and nobody would have been court martialed, because our mission was sanctioned by Covert Ops."

"Explain."

"Are you familiar with a race known as the Berali, Commander?"

"Yes, I have heard of them in passing."

"Hmm," Jason Cobalt mused. "That does seem to be their legacy, doesn't it. It seems almost fitting then that they may pass quietly into the night. Snuffed out by an act of malice so deep, that it could only be brought about at the expense of an entire race." Sorthac didn't follow his meaning. "You see, sir, the Berali and another race called the Empiri were locked in an epic little struggle while we were having our little temper-tantrum with the Crysallis that we refer to grandiosely as 'The Two-Decade War.' Yes, an epic struggle we both were embroiled in, but one key piece of information that you weren't aware of is that during the last five years of the war, the Star Alliance was secretly negotiating with the Berali to help them end the struggle peacefully."

Sorthac stared at Jason. His face was a mask.

"SEAL Team Five was placed there to gather intelligence and also to make sure that at least the Berali, who were apparently willing to cooperate with us, adhered to the tenets of the treaties we tried to work out. From our perspective, the Berali were playing ball. The Empiri, on the other hand, were not so much violating the treaties, but they didn't trust the Alliance Navy, and they didn't trust our motives. These people we xenophobic and they seemed to have a genetic predisposition toward being distrustful of everyone and everything." He paused to lick his lips. "The problem was, Mr. Sorthac, that the Empiri felt they were being handed a loaded deck, and being told to like it, or lump it. They felt that the Star Alliance had a very backhanded approach to dealing with them. They got this crazy notion into their heads that the US was secretly backing the Berali and that we had aligned ourselves with them. The fighting between the two worlds escalated to the point where the Alliance had to pull out to avoid claiming any further involvement. That's when they started developing chemical weapons."

Lt. Martinez gasped in horror. Sorthac reminded himself that she was young and not desensitized to such atrocious occurrences. Sorthac wasn't sure if that was a good or bad thing. Jason continued.

"The Berali had the good sense to develop these weapons in space labs where the testing could be sealed off from the populace. The Empiri, again succumbing to their own xenophobia, tested their weapons on their own homeworld. One day, approximately eighteen months ago, the Empiri had a massive disaster at one of their testing facilities and the entire population of Empiria was wiped out. The war ended on that day."

Lt. Martinez was confused. "Why did it end that day? The Empiri space forces wouldn't have been affected..."

Jason smiled a wry smile. "The young ones never understand," he commented to no one in particular. "Lieutenant, the entire race committed mass suicide after the loss of their homeworld. They believed that a race without a homeworld had no right to exist."

"So if the war is over, and the Empiri are dead, what is this 'billions of lives to save' crap about, sir," Lt. Commander Harrison asked.

"Well, Commander, not all of the Empiri are dead, or were, I daresay. A small team stayed alive in a last ditch effort to destroy their hated enemy. It was a final attempt to bring about the end to their most hated enemy. The Empiri developed a technology that would allow them to seize an entire planet and move it. Specifically, the Empiri used the last remaining resources of their species to redirect a rouge planet to collide with the Berali homeworld."

There were gasps from around the bridge.

"Sir, the Berali have no idea that this fate is about to befall them. The rouge planet has some kind of distortion field dropped around it so that the Berali's primitive scanning equipment can't see it."

Sorthac scratched his scaly brow. "I do not understand. Why isn't the Star Alliance attempting to avert this catastrophe, Commander? Why was it necessary for all of the cloak-and-dagger? Stealing a starship is a treason offense to say the least. So is kidnapping and hostage-taking. Why the clandestine operation?"

"Because, Commander," he explained. "The Star Alliance is being scrutinized heavily by the Crysallis right now. If the SA took any overt action to save the lives of the Berali, it would be considered an act of war by the Crysallis. they have a vested interest in seeing this become neutral space"

"You're losing me," Harrison interjected. "How does the fate of the Berali affect relations between the SA and the Crysallian Collective?"

"The Crysallis consider the Berali to be mortal enemies. Worse than us, even. In spite of their limited technology by comparison, the Crysallis have tried on seventy-five separate occasions in the last five hundred years to overrun the Berali and failed each time." Then as an after thought: "Oh, and the location is a prime strategic location for a space station. The Crysallis don't like the idea of us putting an outpost so dangerously close to their shipyards in the Weibris system."

"So, you're saying that the SA is willing to sacrifice the lives of a few billion Berali to avoid a war? That's ridiculous," Sorthac scoffed.

"Commander, seventy billion died in the war between our peoples five-hundred years ago. One hundred fifty million died in the Border Skirmish War forty years ago and fifty-five million died in the Two-Decade War. We lost more than our fair share in that war alone. I don't think the SA is eager to repeat that holocaust anytime soon. Look at us in this room. Kids and grizzled veterans and nothing in between. It's like this throughout the armed services."

Sorthac seriously considered that as he examined the faces on the bridge. If he hadn't been Chotan, would he be alive today, he wondered.

"So what do we do now, Commander?"

"The original plan was to give the Navy total deniability. If it were a sanctioned operation, it would have meant war for the Star Alliance. But, on the other hand, if it were seen as a rouge operation, perpetrated by a few desperate extremists, the government could sweep it under the rug and the rest of us would slip away quietly into the night. They'd launch an investigation that would turn up nothing, and there would be no hint at an alliance between the SA and the Berali so the Crysallis would basically be happy and the Berali would get to live."

"It sounds like a reasonable enough plan," Sorthac agreed. "But you damaged a lot of Navy property in this little endeavor. We may be able to help you, but I suspect that regardless of the outcome of this operation, your career in the navy is probably over."

"All of the property we destroyed was either slated for demolition, decommissioning or can easily be repaired. So I highly doubt that. Besides: as I said, we're actually on the government's dime."

"So, what do we do now?" Harrison asked.

"I think I have a plan," Sorthac said.

Chapter 8

"Say again, Commander?"

Sorthac cleared his throat and said it again. "I say we complete the mission, sirs." He waited for the full impact of his statement to sink in.

"I thought that the reason the Navy couldn't intervene was that it would start a full scale war, Commander. How does the fact that the ship was stolen alter that fact?" Gil Cobalt wondered.

"If it is not an officially sanctioned operation, then the Navy is only liable for attempting to stop the *Moonhawk* from destroying the rouge planet. The worst case scenario is that the Crysallis suspect us of lying and go to war with us regardless. The best case scenario is that we save three billion inhabitants and the Crysallis simply think that the Navy is incompetent."

Admiral Cobalt scowled. "I don't like either option Mr. Sorthac. Making the Navy look incompetent doesn't help our cause with the Crysallis any more than going to war with them. It simply invites more yahoos like the group that blew up Jupiter Station six months ago to wreak havoc on the fair citizens of the Star Alliance."

Lt. Martinez spoke up this time. "Sir, begging the Admiral's pardon, but we are forgetting that the *Moonhawk* is the single most powerful weapon in the

Navy's arsenal. Failing to stop anyone who manages to capture it would not be perceived as incompetence, and if it was leaked that it was a rouge operation, the Crysallis would suspect that it was pulled off by someone on the inside with sufficient skill and training to execute such an operation."

The senior officers looked at each other evaluating each other's reaction to the young Lieutenant's statement. "It still looks bad that the flagship of the entire fleet was stolen right out of our own backyard even if it was by one of our own." Commander Barker noted.

"Sirs, it is a calculated public relations risk, but what choice do we have?" Lt. Martinez asked.

"I really don't like the fact that Covert Ops arranged this clusterfuck. Remind me to punch Admiral Paladin the next time I see him. We have to set this up to look like we are trying to stop the *Moonhawk* again, and the Marines and SEAL Team Five is going to have to disappear when it is all over. Question is: How do we do it?" Admiral Cobalt asked.

"I think I have an idea, Admiral," Jason Cobalt said. "But we better hurry, we only have a few hours left before the rouge planet reaches the point of no return."

The plan was simple: The *Galahad* and the *Moonhawk* would start shooting their lesser weapons at each other and at the crucial moment where the

Moonhawk would make it's escape, the *Galahad* would eject a bottle of plasma form it's engine exhaust. The shots would hit the bottle causing it to rupture and there would be an explosion. In the ensuing chaos, the *Moonhawk* would slip away and gain the few precious moments necessary to beat the *Galahad* to the scene and destroy the rouge planet.

The plan was brilliant and elegant, thought Jason Cobalt. He checked his readouts again. All of the turrets were showing green on the board. He double-checked all of the firing mechanisms; he didn't want any misfires. That would be disastrous. He looked over to the command center. Captain Ishido Kamazaki had taken command of the *Moonhawk* so he could oversee the fireworks show from this end. Meanwhile, Admiral Cobalt stayed aboard the *Galahad* to keep up appearances. To any onlookers who might be observing this looked like some kind of standoff between the two ships. It was a convincing one at that. The *Moonhawk* had suffered quite a bit of damage in the last four months. Jason had heard Captain Kamazaki comment on a number of occasions since coming aboard that they needed to find a truly secure dry-dock facility so that he could spend the next month overhauling the "beastly ship" (as he put it) in peace. Kamazaki came over to Jason and stood behind him looking at the readings over his shoulder.

"Watch the energy spikes, kid. You'll blow out the whole damn grid," he said. Kamazaki pushed some buttons on the panel and all of the turrets showed blue and the word "ready" beneath them. "If you don't know how to read the boards, you really shouldn't be handling the most critical controls."

Jason just smiled at him. "Well, sir, you got me there. I'm not as familiar with *these* weapon systems. But I bet I could field strip a hundred different weapons that you've never seen before, let alone *used*."

"Remind me never to confuse you for an engineer again, Commander, you had me *completely* fooled," Kamazaki stated dryly.

"I once made a cannon out of a bamboo stalk, rocks and primitive gunpowder made from sulfur and coal," Jason offered.

"Your father must be proud." And with that, Captain Kamazaki went back to preparing for the light show. Jason wondered how his father put up with some of these personalities. Sorthac was all business, but he respected him as a warrior and Harrison, well she was just downright cute as far as Jason Cobalt was concerned. Not that he was actually interested in her, but she was appealing to him at least on a physical level. *Personally, I'm glad there aren't any Outsiders onboard right about now,* Jason thought. *Especially with thoughts like that running through my head.* The communications panel saved him from any more introspective thinking.

"We are a go over here. Do your worst."

"Acknowledged," was Kamazaki's curt

response. "Commander Cobalt, the weapons systems if you please."

Jason Cobalt's hands worked the console. On the outer skin of the ship all of the gun ports turned in the direction of the *Galahad*. The other ship's weapons mirrored the move. There was a tense pause and then:

"Fire!"

The two massive vessels opened up with a firestorm the likes of which Jason Cobalt had never seen before. The blue bolts emanating from the two ships blanketed each other's shields in an iridescent glow.

"Shields holding, Captain. No damage."

"Prepare to bleed off power to the shields until they are twenty percent below maximum capacity. That should effectively convince any potential witnesses that we are actually engaged in a firefight."

"Aye sir," Lt. Martinez responded from tactical.

"Mr. Cobalt, shut down turrets one, six, twelve and twenty-six. We'll be simulating damage."

"Got it, Captain."

"Now all we do is hope that our timing is perfect, or this whole operation will go up in smoke."

The starship *Galahad* started to shake under the barrage. Admiral Cobalt realized it was because the heavy frigate was less than half of the size of the *Moonhawk* but it was still disconcerting. He suspected, however, that it was taking much more of a toll on the younger crew of the *Galahad*. He looked around the bridge of the starship at the faces of her crew. They were al intent on doing a good job, but he could see them shaking a little. It had to be taxing on all of them to be this brave, so young. They were forced to grow up so fast. Almost an entire generation had been lost in the Two-Decade War. Humanity hadn't suffered a loss so great since World War I on the European continent. *Children, all of them,* he thought. *This act we commit today will ensure that such a tragic loss of life won't occur again on my watch.*

"Take turrets four, six and twelve offline. Prepare to eject plasma bottle on my mark," ordered Captain Melissa Cobalt.

"Aye sir. Turrets offline, bottles are prepared."

She hesitated for a brief moment, building up suspense. "Release the bottles now, Lieutenant."

"Aye Captain."

The Lieutenant pressed some buttons on the console and out dropped two magnetic containers filled with engine exhaust. The containment bottles floated away from the frigate several thousand meters per second. One of the ion blasts from the Moonhawk stuck the container and it exploded in a brilliant flash of light. There was a small shockwave that enveloped the rear of the frigate. The ship seemed to disappear from view for a second as the burning gasses surrounded them. Inside the lights began to flicker and some of the panels burst in a shower of sparks.

"Keep us steady, Lieutenant!" Shouted Captain

Cobalt.

The ship continued to rock violently as the young Lieutenant at the helm desperately held on to the wheel trying to keep the ship from going out of control. They rode the shockwave for a few more seconds and almost as quickly it was gone. The crew of the ship looked around at each other like they were amazed to see that they were still alive.

"Sirs, the Moonhawk is gone, unless my sensors are malfunctioning."

"Everything is going according to plan," Melissa Cobalt said. "Prepare to track their course and follow." She then looked at her father accusingly.

"I thought your man said that it was only going to be a fireworks display."

Admiral Cobalt looked at her sheepishly. "I should have known that when Ishido says 'fireworks' it means simply that he was sure we won't be completely destroyed in the process."

She tossed up her hands in resignation. "Commander Barker, I need a shipwide damage report ASAP. You have the bridge."

"Of course Captain," he responded.

"I hope we still have enough ship left to make a convincing show of it," she said and she stormed off the bridge to the conning tower.

"We are clear of the *Galahad*, Captain," Harrison reported.

"Set course to intercept the rouge planet, all ahead emergency speed," Captain Kamazaki responded. She input the coordinates and the ship jumped into dimensional subspace to cover the remaining distance. Captain Kamazaki turned toward Jason Cobalt. "So, explain what exactly we are going to be doing here Commander."

Jason looked uncomfortable for a moment, but he quickly regained his composure. "Well, put simply, we can't just vaporize the entire planetoid because it would break into much smaller pieces and rain down on Beralia. We would strike it with the main tachyon cannon and split the planet in two. Of course, this whole operation is dependent on us arriving in time to blast it in two. The two halves would miss the planet and float harmlessly into space." He waited a few moments for the impact to sink in. "Of course, if we don't get there in time, we won't split the planet in time and the Berali will simply be a memory just like the Empiri."

"So if we don't blow the pieces apart far enough away from the planet, their trajectory will cause them to hit the planet instead," Kamazaki reiterated.

"Essentially. My father is a big twentieth century motion picture fan. He probably would have referred to the PNR as 'zero barrier' if I remember the disaster film correctly." Jason thought that it might be wishful thinking, but he actually thought he saw Kamazaki smile at that last comment. Apparently the late-night twentieth-century film fests were still a Cobalt mainstay. Harrison desperately tried not to look away from the helm for fear of laughing out loud.

"We should run some more simulated projections before we arrive," Sorthac said.

Kamazaki regained his stony face. "Very true Commander. We wouldn't want to miss it. We won't get a second chance."

Chapter 9

It seemed like they had run a million simulations to Harrison. It also felt like they had been traveling for days, the anxiety was building and the tension was palpable. They had actually only been traveling for about three hours, but it may as well have been years to the young Lieutenant Commander. Suddenly she saw it big as day on her scanners. She looked up and strained her eyes to see it through the forward viewports. Rachael had read about them, but she had never seen one before yet there it was right in front of her: a rouge planet.

It looked like any other planet might. It had mountain ranges, deserts valleys and plains, but unlike any other planet, this one had no star and as a result was nothing more than a ball of ice and rock in space. Maybe this planet was a distant planet in a star system that had some catastrophe or maybe it slipped away during that system's formation but there it was looming silently in front of them. Beyond the galactic iceberg's massive visage she could see the lush, green planet Belaria. She imagined the landscape of that world as Jason had described it to her.

Belaria had twin moons that chased each other across the magenta horizon. They called them The Lovers because they spent all of eternity following after one another. Rachael thought that the story was kind of romantic. He also told her about the sunsets there. They were a sight to behold. The explosive cacophony of colors that littered the landscape at sundown was enough to stop the breath in your chest, he had said. And if they didn't stop this miserable little ball of ice, all of that would be destroyed instantly. The people, the culture, the view, all of it would vanish without a trace.

All because of a stupid war that the losers couldn't stand losing, Rachael thought angrily. "Sir, I have the rouge planet in sight," she said.

"Put it on the holo-viewer," Kamazaki said.

The planet came into focus on the holographic viewer. It looked even meaner and uglier up close than it did far away, Harrison thought. Kamazaki edged closer to the image to scrutinize it. After studying it for a few moments he turned to the science station. "Show me grid nine-alpha, Lt. Martinez," he said.

"Aye, sir." She brought the grid in for a closer inspection of the planet. Kamazaki studied the image a little longer.

He pointed to a large craggy mountain range. "Enhance this area."

"Enhancing," she said. The computer filtered the image and gave a clearer picture of what the terrain on the surface was like. Kamazaki apparently found what he was looking for because he turned and pointed at the image.

"Mr. Cobalt, target our main tachyon cannons at

grid nine-alpha. If we strike the planet along that fault line, it should crack like an egg."

"Targeting grid nine-alpha, aye. Acquiring shooting solution."

"Fire when you have a shooting solution."

The massive turrets aimed at the spiraling, dead planet along the fault line trying to line up the shot. The planet was gyrating too much for the automatic targeting system to compensate and an absolutely precise shot was called for.

Jason looked up from the targeting computer at Kamazaki.

"Well, Lt. Commander Cobalt? Why haven't we fired yet?"

"Sir, the planet is wobbling too much. The Tachyon Cannon wasn't designed for a pinpoint strike on a moving target. It was designed for pulverizing other starships or stationary objects. I'm going to have to target it manually, sir."

There was a series of gasps from around the bridge. The Tachyon Cannon was a relatively new technology and as a result it was tricky equipment at best. Additionally, these weapons were massive. Firing it manually was no easy trick indeed. Kamazaki raised his hands calling for quiet.

"Do you think you can do it, Mr. Cobalt?"

Jason hesitated for a moment. "Yes sir. I do."

"Do what you have to then, Mr. Cobalt."

Jason swallowed and tried to clear the butterflies

from his stomach. He found that they only bothered him when he was doing something that had never been attempted before, like stealing the flagship of the fleet, for example. They didn't just show up whenever he was risking his life. That came with the territory. Now he had the lives of billions in his hands. It made him feel powerful and weak at the same time. He thought he was going to lose his lunch.

He adjusted the targeting scanners to line up with the fault line. The planet kept bouncing off the scope as it tumbled through space. For a brief instant he wondered if the massive rock was actually on a collision course at all. Of course, he realized that the only thing that was moving away from the target was his sensors from the crack on the surface of the planet. He steeled himself. *C'mon, C'mon,* he thought to himself. *Line up you bastard!*

He moved the controls left then right. Up then down. The planet was rolling faster that he could compensate for. Closer and closer the rouge planet rolled to Bearia. Jason imagined the looks of horror on the faces of the Belarians in their last few seconds knowing full well that they are about to be pulverized. The fault line rolled into view again and just as he was about to squeeze the trigger it rolled out of view again. *Damnit*, he thought.

Jason quickly scanned the bridge. Rachael was intently riding the helm, trying to keep the massive starship's nose turned toward the rolling rock.

Samantha and Heather Martinez were busily going over the shield output reports. Sorthac was leaning against the tactical station staring at the readouts of the planet, obviously watching for any stray meteorites that would alter the course of the giant projectile. His eyes came to rest on Ishido Kamazaki who was still staring at him. Jason could see in his eyes that his vast patience was wearing thin. And time was running out. Jason turned back to the console and took a deep cleansing breath.

"Some time today would be good, Commander," Captain Kamazaki said evenly.

"Aye sir," Jason replied. *One more turn and I think I've got it,* Jason thought.

The planet seemed to be turning faster. Jason counted of the seconds in his mind. *Five…four… three…two…one…*

The crack came into view and Jason squeezed the trigger. A ferocious bolt ripped from the humungous turret on the bow of the *Moonhawk* and lanced the planet. At first it seemed as though the beam merely went through the planet and came out the other side, but suddenly explosions seemed to rip through its craggy surface. The surface shook violently as the core of the planet spilled forth and the planet blew apart. A ring of fire erupted forth from the center. Molten rock and debris blew outward and stuck the *Moonhawk's* shields as the two halves of the planet moved apart. The skeleton crew watched silently as the two remaining halves continued spreading apart. They were still moving toward Belaria.

"Come on, miss 'em," Harrison said out loud.

The halves kept spreading further apart. *They're not moving fast enough,* Jason thought. The pieces were almost on top of the planet and looked as though they were about to hit.

"Captain, should I move us in to blast one of the other pieces?" Harrison asked.

"Hold on a second, Commander," Kamazaki said.

Jason couldn't keep from fidgeting in his seat. "Sir, if we don't move in…"

"As you were, Mister." There was no edge in his tone.

"But sir, they're gonna…"

But it was too late. The two halves crossed the point of no return… and slid right past Belaria by a mere three hundred miles on either side.

The bridge erupted in cheers.

Ishido Kamazaki let out a sigh of relief. He was really glad he didn't have to explain to Admiral Cobalt why Belaria was a smoldering pile of rubble. But now there was no time for any of that. He turned to Jason Cobalt.

"Mr. Cobalt, I think it is time for you and your team to depart."

"Captain, how will you explain the presence of the marines onboard?"

"I'll invent something," he said and then added

with a wink: "Nice shooting Mr. Cobalt. It's been a pleasure serving with you...under the circumstances."

Lt. Commander Jason Cobalt merely smiled. He looked to his team and in unison they issue a formal salute to the *Moonhawk* crewmembers. The *Moonhawk* crewmembers returned the gesture.

"Good luck, Commander," Harrison said.

"Well met, Harrison. You haven't lost any of your skills. Either as a pilot or as a SEAL." Rachael beamed. With that last comment he bid the crew adieu. Jason, Samantha, and Jerry made their way to the motivator shaft, the doors parted and they disappeared inside.

"Force Recon One to Alpha Leader, we have managed to secure the *Moonhawk* but it seems that the perpetrators have escaped. Awaiting orders."

"Secure all stations and stand by for Admiral Cobalt, Recon One."

"Understood, Alpha Leader."

Admiral Cobalt was the first one on deck when the launch doors opened. It felt good to be back on the deck of his ship, although, he noted that it was a little worse for wear since he had last seen it.

"I apologize for the mess Admiral," Lt. Commander Harrison greeted. "I'm afraid I have to take credit for the damage. There was a firefight and one of the fuel canisters ruptured."

"Well, I think we can forgive you this time,

Commander. At least you didn't blow the entire ship up. I'm putting you up for the Distinguished Service Medal."

"Thank you, sir. But I was just doing my job."

"That's what I always liked about you, Commander. You aren't a glory hound."

Rachael decided to change the subject. "Captain Kamazaki and Commander Sorthac are waiting for you on the bridge, sir. It also appears that one of our shuttles has gone missing, Admiral."

"Missing eh, Commander?" Cobalt grinned knowingly.

"Shuttle one, return to the ship immediately, or we will be forced to fire upon you," Lt. Martinez said into the mouthpiece." Admiral Cobalt and Lt. Commander Harrison arrived on the bridge just in time to witness this odd spectacle.

"Never," came the badly garbled reply. "We will never surrender to you imperialistic pigs! We would rather die in space, sucking vacuum rather than surrendering to the likes of you."

Cobalt smiled to himself. *He's laying it on thick*, he thought. But the 'imperialistic pigs' remark was a bit much.

"The Brotherhood for the Freedom of Worlds will never surrender to the Star Alliance," the voice continued over the speakers. *'The Brotherhood' no less*, thought Cobalt. Cobalt decided to play his part.

"This is Admiral Gilliad Cobalt. You have no hope of escape. Terrorism against the United Star Alliance will not be tolerated. Surrender now, and we may show leniency." Gil Cobalt was satisfied with himself. *It sounded so good, I almost convinced myself,* he thought.

Suddenly there was an explosion and the tiny craft disappeared in a flash of light. A small shockwave shook the *Moonhawk* slightly and then there was nothing but the image of Belaria and open space in the viewport.

Oh, my God, Jason--, Cobalt thought frantically. "What the hell just happened," Cobalt demanded. "Who fired that shot?!"

"Admiral!"

Cobalt turned toward the tactical station where the shout came from. Ensign Ellery who was manning the post looked stricken. "Sir, it's a *Bre' Telk* class Crysalian Cruiser!"

"Condition red, communications, warn that ship off! Give me shields, now!"

The massive Crysalian battlecruiser came into the forward viewport of the *Moonhawk*. Cobalt always thought they were creepy because they looked more like they were 'grown' in a lab like the experiments he did with crystals at the academy rather than built. Upon closer inspection the menacing starship with its severe crystalline structure would never be mistaken for a rock drifting through space. There was form, structure, and even an odd symmetry to the bizarre rock ship. Like the linear particle cannons that protruded from the flanks of the massive ship. The *Bre'Telk* class was a mere baby step behind the *Moonhawk* in raw firepower, which is what made them such a threat during the war. They sliced up the powerful, but flawed *Kevlar* class on a regular basis.

"Sir, they are hailing us!"

This caught Admiral Cobalt off guard. Normally the Crysallis didn't call to negotiate so quickly after the kill. Rage and despair nearly boiled over in Admiral Cobalt. *How dare they call me to gloat after murdering my son and his crew*, he fumed. And after such an insignificant infraction, too.

"Put those murdering sons-of-bitches on the screen."

"Aye, sir," the ensign almost whispered.

The craggy face of the Crysalian captain appeared on the screen. Cobalt expected to see a smug or at least condescending expression on the captain's face, but instead he thought he detected a hint of disappointment in his counterpart's face.

"It is regrettable that I was forced to do that, Admiral Cobalt. I expected more form you."

Cobalt's eyes blazed. "You had no right to interfere with Star Alliance official business. We had the situation under control!"

"I don't think so Admiral. If you had the situation under control, the perpetrators would not have been escaping.   You also would not have been threatening to destroy them if they failed to comply. Crysalian justice is swift and direct. Any act of treason is handled with extreme prejudice, Admiral."

"Right, like the time that terrorists from that fringe group bombed Jupiter Station and killed twenty thousand Alliance citizens and your government swore that they were 'radicals' and would be dealt with swiftly," Admiral Cobalt retorted.   "By the way, Captain, how is that investigation proceeding?"

The Crysalian captain shifted uncomfortably in his seat.   "The treaty accord specifically labels this planet as 'off limits' to all parties, Admiral. I suggest that since you obviously have regained control of your ship you leave this sector within the next eleven standard hours or the treaty will be in abeyance."

With that last comment his image winked out of existence and the visage of the alien starship returned to the screen.   The massive enemy battlecruiser turned slowly and broke orbit. After a few moments the ship distorted and slipped into hyperspace.

"Set a course for the waystation in the Verisus system, Ensign.   Communications, signal the *Galahad* and tell them to meet us there."

"Aye, sir."

"Course laid in, sir."

"Get us out of here."

Admiral Cobalt could barely contain his grief toward the death of his only son, and only a few years ago he lost Jason's mother. He wondered what he would tell Jason's sisters about his death. Melissa would be professional about it, but Skye; she was still pretty young. She looked up to her older brother. He looked at Neriah Solis for a moment. She started to say something, but she was interrupted by the sound of clapping. Gil swung around to see Jason and his mates Sam and Jerry standing on the bridge in their standard issue blues, grinning like idiots. Cobalt felt the jubilation bubble up within him to see his son standing there, alive. He quickly made his way across the bridge to where they were standing and grabbed his son by the shoulders as though he would hug him. At the last second he thought better of it in light of the fact that only his youngest officers were present on the bridge.

"H-how--?" he stammered. Gil found himself grinning like an idiot, too.

"It's the old bait and switch. A classic execution, if I do say so," Jason smiled.

"Well, you obviously weren't on the shuttle..."

"Well, Admiral, it's simple. We were controlling the shuttle remotely from the Moonhawk. The Crysallis were fooled into believing that we were onboard because we used a device that creates false life signs. We call them 'Life Spoofers' in the field," Samantha explained.

"She's the tech wizard," Jason noted. "I don't pretend to understand all of this stuff, but unless the Crysallis go back and scan the area for biological material in the wreckage of the shuttle, they will think that they destroyed the so-called terrorists.

"But... why?"

Jason shifted his weight as if he was in distress.

"I'm sorry to put you through that, sir. But we've been tracking that Crysallis ship for a while. We knew if we were going to make good our escape, we had to convince them that your grief was sincere."

Gilliad Cobalt contemplated this new information, but quickly his smile returned and he clapped his son on the shoulder in admiration.

"Well, you sure fooled me. And that's no easy task, son."

Epilogue

Captain Melissa Cobalt was leaning against the wall when Admiral Gil Cobalt came out of the conference room. He was the last one to file out. She straightened up and waited for the other officers to be clear of earshot before she spoke to her father. Admiral Cobalt saw her and spoke first.

"Oh, hey Melissa. We were just finalizing our statements for the mission report. What're you doing here? I thought you had returned to your ship."

"That was unfair what you tried to do to Neriah, sir. I could tell that you were trying to have her 'handle' me back on the *Galahad*… when I was being obstinate."

"I didn't—"

She stopped him in mid-sentence by raising her hand. "Don't bullshit me now, dad. I saw that staying hand on her shoulder. The bridge of my ship, or your ship, or anywhere public for that matter is inappropriate for settling our differences."

He pierced her with his stare. She jumped back a little, startled. He took her roughly by the arm and pulled her into the corridor junction.

"First of all, don't forget that we are still Navy officers and that we are still on the deck of a Navy vessel, so drop the familiar in front of the crew." His look softened a little, he looked more tired that angry.

"Second of all, you're right." She looked at him strangely, like she wasn't sure that she heard him correctly.

"Yes, you heard correctly. It was an imposition on my friendship with her and it was inappropriate for me to ask her to act in an official capacity to resolve our personality conflicts."

"She looked like she was going to blow her stack," Melissa commented.

"Don't worry about her. I'll make it up to her in my own way."

"Well, what about Jason. What will become of him," she asked almost conspiratorially.

"Well, I can't think of a much worse punishment than forcing him to return to Admiral Paladin's command. That's the price of 'following orders'."

Lieutenant Commander Jason Cobalt stood at attention in his father's office. He half expected him to lob a pulse grenade over the desk at him, but he showed no outward sign that he was prepared for the worst. It was an unusual fashion of torture to have his old man simply sitting there going over his personnel record, quietly. After what seemed like an eternity, Admiral Cobalt flipped the file shut and lobbed it onto the desk. He looked up solemnly at his son.

"I'm not happy about all this deception. It's one of the primary reasons I left Covert Operations in the first place. I'm even less happy about the fact that my son is now a part of that life," Admiral Cobalt said.

"You always told me I needed to find my own way. It just so happened that path coincided with yours, sir."

Admiral Cobalt was nonplussed. He stood up from his desk and paced with his hands clasped behind his back.

"Don't get me wrong. Macia Paladin and I have been friends for the better part of my adult life. But I will not hesitate to tell anyone that I disapprove of his tactics and methods, even though I chimed in and voted for him to take this job when Colson disgraced himself."

"I'm not married to the guy, Dad. But in this case, he was right."

Admiral Cobalt stops pacing and looks sharply at his son. He then looked away at the stars outside his window with a solemn expression on his face.

"Yes, he was. This time."

Commodore Neriah Solis was already standing at her customary station beside the holographic map table when Gil Cobalt arrived on the bridge. He strode over to stand at her side and placed both hands on the table in front of him. She looked over at him and smiled.

"Admiral, Verisus Station signals that they have completed the supply transfer and that we are cleared for departure."

"Well, what do you think about a nice long

layover in a traditional spacebound shipyard, Neriah?"

"I think that sounds like a capital idea, Captain."

"Mister Harrison, set course for the Selenius system, best speed if you please."

Harrison smiled back at the admiral from the helm. "Selenius system, aye-aye, sir. You heard the man, Martinez. Let's punch it."

"Aye aye, Ops," came Martinez's jovial reply.

Admiral Cobalt stepped back from the table and crossed his arms. *That which doesn't kill us makes us stronger*, he mused.

In space, the *Moonhawk* arced around and dove into the shining portal in the darkness, of to adventures yet untold.

Glossary of Terms

USAS
United Star Alliance Ship

Pulse Rifle
Primary hand-assault weapon of the Star Alliance. It fires charged particle beams at high velocity toward the target.

Navy SEAL's
Named in honor of the United States Navy Special Forces Group of our time of the same name. The acronym stands for "Sea Air Land". The term is a bit anachronistic in the 30th Century, but their function is essentially the same.

Tachyon Cannon
Ultra-powerful weapon on the Moonhawk. The name is a misnomer as it does not fire actual tachyons, but more accurately, describes the massive particle weapon's power source. It has the power to cleave a planet in half. Or simply obliterate it.

How to Steal a Starship

The History of the Future:

Humankind burst onto the galactic scene in the early 22nd Century. However, it was not a joyous time as corporate greed and massive, unmanageable syndicates had taken over all aspects of human life, rendering the world governments ineffective. These Megacorporations took the defense of Earth and space exploration away from the military and began to operate under their own "Manifest Destiny". Shortly after humanity breached Interstellar Space beyond the Oort Cloud and began colonizing planets in nearby star systems, the Megacorporations ran afoul of a brutally efficient warrior race known as The Chotan. The lizard-like Chotan took an instant dislike to the duplicitous nature of human business practices and declared war on our entire species and way of life. The Megacorps. severely squandered and mismanaged the war and as a result, humanity suffered incalculable losses in life and resources. Humanity surrendered to the Chotan in the mid-22nd Century and ended up being a slave race to the mighty Chotan for over two centuries.

In the late 2400's, humanity finally grew weary of their oppression and began pockets of resistance at great cost over the Chotan overlords. Rumors began to circulate that a freedom fighter known only as "*Moonhawk*" had scored several key victories and served as a catalyst to spark a full-blown revolution. The Chotan Empire had subjugated a great many races under their scaly thumbs and as a result they had no shortage of enemies among the "chattel" races. With the legend of "*Moonhawk*" growing and more and more victories came pouring in, additional races joined the human effort to overthrow their oppressors. By 2492, 13 different species in total rallied under Moonhawk's banner and in short order, the Chotan were defeated; pushed back to their home space.

The *United Star Alliance* was founded one year after the Armistice in 2493. Under the latin slogan "*Nunquam iterum*" ("Never again"), the *Star Alliance* set about to the task of freeing the subjugated races across the galaxy as well as gaining new allies and strengthening their perimeter against future attack. Aside from a multitude of minor conflicts with the Chotan resulting from centuries of enmity, the next 400 years mark a period of mutual growth for the Alliance and its members, as well as a successful defense of their borders and expansion via exploration. The Alliance even befriended an ancient and extremely powerful race of humanoids known as The *Zendosians* during this time. *Zendosians* are a "Type II" galactic civilization, meaning that they have managed to develop the technology to use the entire power output of their solar system. "*Zendosia Prime*" is not so much a planet as it is a *Dyson Sphere* built around their home star to utilize 100% of its power output. *Zendosia* did spare the second planet of their solar system due to an indigenous race of people believed to be *Zendosia's* ancient progenitors. The second planet orbits their home star inside their protective *Dyson Sphere* and is considered a sacred Holy Land with relics that pre-date the *Zendosian's* 250,000 years of space travel. Their home base (the Sphere itself) is codenamed by the Alliance as "*Space Station Alexandria*", in reference to Alexander the Great's capital city, one of the high points of ancient human civilization.

In the 2860's, Humanity began expansion into the Orion Arm of the Galaxy. It was at this point that humans first encountered the nomadic *Crysallis*. The *Crysallis* moved in convoys and observed no interstellar borders. This mentality began countless eons ago when their ancestral home planet was destroyed by a foreseen cataclysm. The *Crysallis* avoided extinction by forging ahead out into the universe with massive space arks called "worldships". Within the worldships, each faction of the *Crysallis* (denoted by primary and secondary colors on the color wheel such as red, blue, yellow, green, orange and purple) preserved different aspects of the environment and culture of their race. A seventh ark belonging to an unknown faction was lost in space countless millennia ago and is believed to have evidence of the Exodus of the Crysallian people into space. Additionally, it contains a supremely ancient set of relics known as "*The Great Statues of Old*" (a common epitaph of the *Crysallis* as well) believed to represent the lost gods of their people.

Due to the lack of centralization, and the utter lack of adherence to any kind of treaties established between various factions and the Star Alliance, the United Star Alliance Galactic Senate declared war on the *Crysallis* in the Spring of 2951. This led to the beginning of *The Two Decades War* between the *Star Alliance* and the newly formed *Crysallian Collective*. Ironically, the *Star Alliance's* declaration of war over the lack of centralization and piracy between the *Crysallian* factions led to the formation of a formal alliance between said factions and the *Crysallis* became a highly focused military machine, thwarting the *Star Alliance* at every turn. This was an unacceptable scenario because the *Star Alliance* suddenly found themselves ill equipped to handle this new superpower, especially since they had just come off fighting the *Chotan* in one, final, cataclysmic battle that terminated the *Chotan Empire* in 2945. Even though the newly reorganized *Chotan Confederation* government sided with the Star Alliance in this conflict, the damage was done, and the *Star Alliance* and its allies limped along for over 20 years attempting to stymie the war machine of the *Crysallian Collective*.

On the eve of April 9, 2968, Captain Gilliad Cobalt arrived at *Star Alliance Naval Command* with a proposal for a mega weapon known as the **Tachyon Cannon**. The

technology was based on the idea of focusing the
energies created by their existing drive technology into
one, massive, fatal burst of power directed forward at a
target. Previously, the *Star Alliance's* attempts at taking
down a *Crysallis* worldship and ending the conflict
resulted in the discovery that an entire star fleet could
not generate enough power with conventional weapons
to crack these mobile fortresses. With the advent of
Tachyon Wave Technology, it became possible to deliver
a power burst at a concentrated point that was
geometrically more powerful than any weapons the
Alliance had used prior. *Central Command* approved the
plan unanimously and Cobalt spent the next 5 years
building the ship codenamed "Moonhawk" in secret.

As with all great military secrets, the enemy somehow
got wind of it and declared peace. So on August 29,
2973 (Starchrono 2973.695, New Earth Calendar), the
Star Alliance and the *Crysallian Collective* entered into
armistice and have been wary neighbors ever since.
Cobalt, being a tenacious engineer and tactician,
persuaded the *Central Command* to let him repurpose
Project Moonhnawk into a battleship, and see the
construction to completion, thus bringing us to the
present shown in my novel "*The Fire and the Forge*".

Side note: thanks to the *Chotan* keeping most subject
races (specifically the slave workforces) naked in pens
for two centuries, modern human society shows a

marked indifference to public nudity. Clothes and uniforms are worn because it is proper decorum (And some non-humanoid species still have taboos against traipsing around in the buff for no reason). However, human morality in the 30th Century is more secular and there are no public indecency laws prohibiting non-sexual nudity. It's not considered strange for the higher echelons of society to host gatherings, parties and social functions completely in the nude. Uninvited groping and fondling, however, is still considered taboo, hence why many of the characters react poorly to having their private parts touched casually in the novels and comics.

The Main Characters:

Commodore/Admiral Gilliad Cobalt - Age: 83 (appears about 40) height: 6'4" - Born in Nova Scotia, Canada, Cobalt was a combat pilot in his early years. During the Chotan war, he was injured so severely that he was no longer able to fly, so after jockeying a desk for a while, he was recruited into Covert Ops by then Captain Torrance Colson. He distinguished himself in secret during this time earning many awards he cannot display. However, some years into this he met his wife Sarah and they began a family. Due to the dubious nature of the work Covert Ops carried out and the low life expectancy of its members, Cobalt transferred to the command tract and served as captain of the *Indefatigable* (the ship named after Horatio Hornblower's famous command, affectionately known as the "Indie"). When his youngest daughter, Skye, was 12 years old, she was critically wounded and blinded in an attack by the Crysallis. Sarah died in this attack, saving Skye's life. Cobalt was never really the same after this. He was moody and made tough calls that lacked in compassion. Lacking, that is, until he was assigned a fresh-faced young Lt. Commander Neriah Natsuke Solis as his first officer. They had a torrid romance behind closed doors, but when circumstances forced Cobalt to make another one of his infamous "tough calls", it put strain on their relationship. Cobalt resigned his command and transferred to Jupiter Outpost so he could oversee Research and Design, and this is where we find him at the outset of the series, developing his new dreadnaught. Cobalt has 3 known children at the outset of the series. His family has a 500 year military tradition dating to the founding of the *Star Alliance* and is considered "military royalty".

Captain/Commodore Neriah Natsuke Solis - Age: 56 (appears between 25-30) - Solis was born in Argentina to a Spanish/Argentinian diplomat (father) and a Japanese/American interpreter (mother). However, her ethnic makeup is not nearly as interesting as another quirk of genetics: Solis is a metahuman known as an "Outsider" (a group of people named after the book by S.E. Hinton for their fringe status having psychic powers). By the 30th Century, the Outsiders have become accepted as oracles and sages of the Star Alliance because, despite extreme prejudice in the early days of the Alliance, they have always been stalwart defenders. Solis is no exception to that and takes her role as a Defender of Peace very seriously. She is sardonic and witty; passionate and elegant. Solis' main role aboard the Moonhawk is as Executive Officer and, because of her combat experience as a pilot, she serves as Commander Air Group (CAG), flying the *Spectre F-505 Space Superiority Fighter*. She is fiercely loyal to Cobalt (and may even still harbor feelings for him in spite of their breakup 25 years ago), but she also frequently challenges him, acting as his voice of conscience and compassion. She is the perfect counterpoint to both his ego and brutal efficiency. Because of her convictions, she frequently acts without fear and is well respected by the crew... except Sorthac...

Commander Sorthac ni'Siissreth - Age: Mid-80's (by human reckoning), Height: 7'4", Species: Chotan - Sorthac is not here entirely of his own accord. At the end of the last war with the Chotan, a portion of the Armistice was a permanent cultural exchange; basically, volunteers were chosen as permanent hostages. They would integrate into the other side's society essentially never to return home on a permanent basis. Sorthac was a well regarded prince with no direct line to the throne of the Empire, and with the Empire's dissolution, he found himself without title or purpose. So, he was one of the first to volunteer. The Chotan are a noble warrior race, and Sorthac is often the epitome of descriptor. However he does harbor bitterness over his change in status and in spite of being lauded for his multitude of victories during the various campaigns he fought for the Star Alliance, has had relatively slow advancement and a deep struggle to find his place among his uneasy human comrades. He is an exemplary officer, driven by his instinctual understanding of his Warrior Code and serves as Security Chief aboard the *Moonhawk*. His record would be virtually unblemished if not for a conflict of personality with first officer Neriah Solis.

Lt. Commander Rachael Harrison - Age 40 (appears 20-22), Red hair, Green eyes. Freckles, Height: 5'4" Lt. Commander Harrison is a top grade officer, given her short stature and comparatively brief career. But, in her years in the service, she has seen much. She began her career during the Two Decade War at its most fearsome height. Star Alliance losses were becoming staggering. She enlisted the instant she was legally able and jumped immediately into the fray as a "Navy SEAL" (Naval Special Forces) and served as a shuttle pilot, ferrying everything from Marine troops to important dignitaries into some of the most dangerous territory in known space. In one incident that the Star Alliance quietly refers to as "Little Bighorn 2", the Alliance 7th fleet was lured into one of the most spectacular ambushes in human military history. All forces would have been lost if Harrison, flying a shuttle towing a massive payload of explosives, hadn't flown into the path of the lead battleship, slinging her load at it in a hairpin turn. The resulting explosion annihilated the dreadnaught and caught the Crysallis so off guard that they broke off their attack and the Shattered 7th Fleet slipped away by jumping a brown dwarf star. Harrison's shuttle was caught in the resulting shockwave that also destroyed several other smaller warships, and after losing all power, she drifted lifeless in space for seven days. Surviving by portioning her combat rations and "recycling" her own water, she was picked up by a Free Trader that was cruising through the system pillaging the debris field. After a fight that nearly cost her her life (and most assuredly resulted in the deaths of all 4 of the traders), she escaped back to Alliance territory. By this point in her career, she had risen to Chief Warrant Officer 3 (after a meteoric rise through the enlisted ranks). In addition to the Star Alliance Medal of Honor, for her conduct and valor, she was given an instant commission at the equivalent commissioned rank of Lieutenant, indefinite leave, and choice of any duty station she wanted in the Known Universe upon her return. Rather than wait, she insisted on being assigned to the *Moonhawk*, the "*Biggest Gun in the Galaxy*", under the command of Commodore Gilliad Cobalt. Cobalt and Harrison share a mentor/menteé relationship and off duty, she refers to him as "Uncle Gilliad".

How to Steal a Starship

Captain Ishido Kamazaki - Age 59 (appears about 35), Japanese ethnicity, black hair, brown eyes, Height: 5'8" - The Chief Engineer of the Moonhawk is jovial, but blunt. He says exactly what is on his mind, consequences be damned (most of the time. He's not completely apolitical). Hand-picked by Commodore Cobalt to lead the design engineering team of the Moonhawk, he was always intended to be the chief engineer on the maiden voyage of the massive vessel and reveled in the idea of being in command of the engine room of the flagship of the fleet. He is loyal and dependable. Initially strangers, he and Cobalt became fast friends due to the large degree of trust Cobalt invested in him. As a result, he is almost unshakably loyal. However, during the events in "The Fire and the Forge", Kamazaki realizes just how impulsive Cobalt can be when he thinks he is right and initially doubts his friend. He comes to realize that doubt is misplaced and for some time, he feels guilt for not trusting Cobalt's uncanny ability to read a situation. He's not the kind to repeat a mistake and occasionally derides himself for this moment of weakness. Kamazaki is quietly gay and shares a lot of time with the much more flamboyantly queer Lt. Colin "Cubby" Parsons, his assistant chief engineer.

Doctor/Captain Heather Lopez - Age 60 (appears around 35), Texan-American + Mexican + Humanoid Alien, Auburn hair, bronze complexion, vibrant aquamarine eye color (from her alien side); Height: 6' - Dr. Lopez is the ship's Chief Medical Officer. She is a kindly doctor, but she often has a crass disposition, acting frequently "put upon" by her shipmates (she secretly adores her companions and worries about them non-stop; she's the "Tsundere" character if this were traditional anime, except nobody is fooled by her attitude). Dr. Lopez came to the *Moonhawk* via the tragedy outlined in the beginning of "*The Fire and the Forge*". The space station she was in command of was attacked and destroyed; her crew murdered in front of her. She would have abandoned the service entirely if not for the kind twist of fate that caused Admiral Cobalt to be her rescuer. Thanks to their history, he was able to convince Heather to stay in the service and work aboard the *Moonhawk* under his command. Lopez is also fiercely loyal and protective of the crew, often acting as a "den mother" to the senior staff and powerful moral compass, in spite of her facade of indifference.

Commander Jono Ardenz - Age: 100+ (actual age uncertain; appears to be 25-30) Species: Beta Centaurian, Height: 5'11" - Jono is the "odd man out". As science officer on a military vessel, he is in a rough spot because he is forced to bridge the gap between being an officer and wrangling the civilian staff aboard the *Moonhawk*, as well as heading the entire Computer Sciences division, being an expert in all-things-A.I. and sending all command-level messages (which annoys the hell out of him because he's the science officer, not the damn communications officer, dammit!). Because Ardenz is assigned all of the tasks that the military officers aboard the ship really don't understand, he frequently feels put-upon and that they really don't appreciate what his job is supposed to be. This causes him to have the schizophrenic attitude of being jovial one minute, and completely disaffected/indifferent (if not outright hostile) the next. Not only all of that, but humans seem to harbor a degree of prejudice against Beta Centaurians for reasons hat are not entirely clear. It could be their finely tuned telepathy linking them to the more salacious actions of the *Outsiders*, causing a fear reaction at the heart of the matter. In any case, in spite of this frustration, Jono understands the real importance of what he does and is devoted to Cobalt because Cobalt recognizes his brilliance and specifically requested his presence on his command. As a result, he is willing to put up with actions above and beyond what is considered "reasonable" for his commanding officer. (Note: Ardenz has a special uniform denoting his position in the Sciences Division. This visual distinction often serves to amplify the divide between him and the rest of the crew. Let it be known that if he had a choice in the matter, he would ask NOT to be different, as it is his fervent desire to fit in with the crew)

Follow the Adventures of the *Starship Moonhawk*™ on the Web!

http://www.starshipmoonhawk.com

Also, find out more about *Moonhawk Publishing* and their latest releases! The mission begins now for in the distant future, one ship stands between order and chaos™ !